Thresl Chronicles

I love getting my little book loving hands on something unique. That is exactly what Amber Kell has given readers with the Thresl Chronicles... Soldier Mine and the world it is centered around are vastly interesting. There is so much that has yet to been uncovered. I am looking forward to moving on in this series. ~ *The Jeep Diva*

If you like paranormal stories with a 'different' type of shapeshifter, a bit of mystery and intrigue and two very hot men falling in love while fighting for their lives, and if you're looking for a mix between heat and a fascinating, different world, then you will probably like this story. ~ *Rainbow Book Reviews*

This story took on a life of its own as it unfolded. The idea of placing someone into stasis to save their lives has been developed into different sci-fi stories, but what was fascinating was the need to find a mate for a Thresl before awakening them. It had to be difficult for Beleine and Sarler to be forced to mate without knowing anything about each other. I was amazed how empaths were used as caretakers for the sleeping Thresl. Sarler's desire to find the perfect mate for his sleeping Thresl showed what an incredible man he was. Many people feel lost when dealing with the emotions of others, like Sarler, but in the end, he proved he could fight for his man. There are many secrets that have yet to be revealed and I for one can't wait! ~ *Fallen Angel Reviews*

This sequel is fascinating... If you like paranormal stories with a 'different' type of shapeshifter, tons of secrets and some intricate court politics, and two hot men falling in love while trying to figure out if that is what they want, and if you're looking for a fascinating, different world, then you will probably like this story. ~ *Rainbow Book Reviews*

THRESL CHRONICLES
Volume One

Soldier Mine

Prince Claimed

AMBER KELL

Thresl Chronicles Volume One
ISBN # 978-1-78184-634-6
©Copyright Amber Kell 2013
Cover Art by Posh Gosh ©Copyright 2013
Interior text design by Claire Siemaszkiewicz
Total-E-Bound Publishing

Published in 2013 by Total-E-Bound Publishing, Think Tank, Ruston Way, Lincoln, LN6 7FL, United Kingdom.

.

SOLDIER MINE

Dedication

To my science fiction fans who enjoy a little man love
in their space adventures.

Chapter One

"Just who I wanted to see."

Kreslan Piers didn't need to turn around to know who had sneaked up behind him in the hall. Barley Tankis' voice haunted his dreams. The bastard had made it his mission in life to bother Kres since basic training. Unfortunately, Barley's father was an admiral in the fleet, so complaining about Tankis' behaviour never produced any results. Kres had learnt that lesson the hard way and had a scar on his arm to show for his efforts.

"Hello, Barley." Kres reluctantly turned to meet his nemesis.

"Hello, faggot," Barley sneered. If his usual expression wasn't so unpleasant, the tall blond could have been considered handsome with his wide shoulders and icy blue eyes. Unfortunately, it didn't take much digging to find the vast ugliness that lay beneath the surface.

"What do you want?" Kres had just finished sixteen hours of guard duty after one of his co-workers had come down with a cold. He could barely keep his eyes open. He didn't need to put up with Barley's crap on top of everything else. He longed for a few hours of sleep followed by a trip to the bar to grab a willing bedmate for a round of stress-reducing sex. Hell, at this point he was so desperate he might even be willing to consider a woman.

"I talked to Sergeant Wallace, and he agreed with me that you should guard the creatures tonight."

Kres' stomach churned over Barley's smug expression.

Shit. So much for stress reduction.

Even though he knew it was pointless, he offered a token protest. "I can't guard them tonight. I just got off sixteen hours. I'm going to get some food, then go to sleep."

Fuck, he needed sleep.

"So I should go back and tell the sergeant you're ignoring a direct order?" Barley's cold eyes glowed with malice.

Anger pulsed through Kres. He knew he was powerless but that didn't stop him from issuing a threat that would no doubt go unfulfilled. "One of these days you're going to get what's coming to you."

He had to believe that. It was the only thing that kept him from punching Barley in the face and getting court-martialled.

With a final glare at Barley, Kres turned and headed towards the cargo bay.

"Enjoy your shift." Barley's mocking laughter followed him down the hall.

Kres wished he could get away with punching the bastard again, but the last time he'd done that, he had been the one who had ended up in the brig for three days while Barley had roamed free. Kres had learnt his lesson. He only did things to Barley when he knew he could get away with them.

Sergeant Wallace gave him a cool look when he arrived. "Took you long enough to get here."

"I came as soon as I heard you wanted me on guard duty, Sergeant. I just got off a double shift." Kres didn't bother to hide the annoyance in his voice. His feet hurt, his back ached and he longed for his hard cot of a bed with a fierce need. At this point, a trip to the brig would at least allow him to get some sleep.

"Then you shouldn't have volunteered for this one," the sergeant barked at him.

"I didn't, Sergeant," Kres replied through gritted teeth.

"Are you saying Barley is a liar?"

How he longed to say yes.

"I would never say that, Sergeant. But then, as I didn't volunteer and Barley said you insisted I do this watch, I'll let you make the judgement call."

The older man gave him a long, considering gaze. "I like Admiral Tankis. Too bad his son is a prick. Unfortunately, because you were volunteered, I let my other guard go. I'm going to need you to take this shift, soldier, and then I'll make sure Barley takes the next three."

The thought of Barley watching animals for one evening much less three drained away most of Kres' anger. "I'll do my duty."

The sergeant slapped Kres on the back, almost knocking the wind out of him. "I knew I could count on you. You're a good man, Piers."

Kres didn't think a good man would enjoy the thought of his enemy's punishment, but he wasn't going to argue. "What do I need to do?"

"Keep an eye out that no one bothers the animals. Check on them if they make any noise. There's been word that someone might be after the Thresl before he makes it to Callavar." The sergeant pointed towards the huge cage in the corner.

Kres nodded. "I'll keep a close watch on him."

Thresls were rare shape-shifters—cat hybrids—that, once bonded with their owners, could take any form. However, the beasts were picky about who they bonded with and often wouldn't stay with their owner if the Thresl found them unworthy. That fact didn't stop black market thieves from snatching the creatures whenever they could. The rich considered owning a Thresl prestigious and would pay outrageous amounts to have one of their own, even if they had to keep it in a cage for the rest of its life. Kres felt sorry for the beasts.

After the sergeant had left, Kres walked amongst the rows of cages, peeking through the grates. Most of the creatures were sleeping. A low growl had him walking towards the Thresl's cage, sweeping his flashlight back and forth to see if there was a reason behind the animal's noises or if simple restlessness made it pace.

Careful to keep his steps quiet in case an intruder was hidden in the hold, Kres approached the Thresl's location. A quick glance around showed no one immediately near the enormous cage. To be thorough, Kres walked all the way around the container. Unable to resist, he peeked inside. A pair of gold eyes peered back. Kres respectfully kept his distance. He'd heard about these creatures mauling people through the bars. The new criss-cross caging supposedly prevented that, but he wasn't taking any chances.

"I don't see anything, pretty kitty," Kres crooned to the animal. As if intrigued by his voice, the large cat moved closer to the latched door. The beast's red and black markings shifted beneath the shadows and limited lighting. Unless there was active loading or unloading, they kept the lights low in the cargo hold in order to preserve power.

The cat gave another growl.

Kres spread his empty hands to show he meant no harm. "I'm not going to mess with you. I've heard how dangerous you are." He stepped back from the cage and looked around. Nothing.

The animal made a low purring noise. Curious, Kres peeked inside again.

"You sure are a pretty thing."

"Talking to the animals now, are we?"

Kres spun around.

Barley and two of his goons, Stanner and Philson, smiled at him, but the look in their eyes was anything but friendly.

"What do you want, Barley?" Kres looked back and forth between the three men. He knew in his gut that this time they meant to do more than just a little harassment. He could almost feel the antagonism pouring off Barley.

"You told Sergeant Wallace I volunteered you," Barley accused.

"You did."

"Why can't you just take your punishment like a man?"

"Because you aren't supposed to be fucking punishing anyone. You think you can do anything you like, but you're just an asshole with a father who gets you out of trouble."

It was like an alien had taken over his mouth and was making him blurt out things he was definitely going to pay for later. Why couldn't he shut the hell up?

"Grab him," Barley ordered.

Barley's goons each took one of Kres' arms and slammed him against the Thresl's cage.

Kres wasn't the type to go down without a fight. Using the goons as leverage, he jumped up and kicked Barley in the face. A satisfying crunch echoed in the hold. Kres smiled at the thought of breaking Barley's nose.

"You bastard! I'm gonna kill you now!" Barley screamed.

Blood poured down Barley's face as he pulled back his arm. He slammed down his fist, evidently intent on doing as much damage as possible, but Kres ducked and Barley hit the metal bars of the cage. Barley screamed with pain as his fingers crashed into the iron rods.

"I said hold him!" Barley shouted.

Stanner and Philson pinned Kres tighter against the Thresl's cage. Kres knew this time there was no getting out of it.

Bracing his body to take Barley's punch, Kres was unprepared for the door at his back to swing inward. Two clawed hands slashed out, swiping long bloody trails across both of the men holding Kres. Blood splashed out of their wounds as they screamed in pain.

Barley's eyes rolled in panic. With a low, savage roar, the Thresl jumped at Kres, shoving him to one side. For a brief, frightening moment he could feel the beast's large fangs at his throat. Turning his head,

Kres bared his throat, freezing his movements and hoping the animal could sense that he meant no harm.

This was it, his last few seconds of life.

Yet, despite Kres' dire predictions, the Thresl licked a spot on his neck then leapt at Barley. With vicious precision, the creature lacerated Barley's face with his claws, leaving bloody trails in their wake.

Kres raced past the shouting men to reach the intercom. Pressing the button, he yelled into the receiver, "Emergency on the cargo deck! Emergency!"

A high-pitched scream pierced the air as Barley fell beneath the Thresl's wrath.

"Shit! No. Don't kill him," Kres commanded.

To his surprise, the creature froze. Leaning over Barley, he bared his fangs. Long and curved, they were razor sharp and dripping with saliva.

Barley let out a whimper as his men cowered in the corner as far from the Thresl as they could get. The creature was blocking their escape route, and neither of them was in any condition to battle a Thresl.

Before Kres could think of what to do, a squad of soldiers rushed onto the cargo deck. Weapons raised, they surrounded the Thresl.

"Don't shoot him!" Kres shouted. "He was protecting me."

Instinct had Kres stepping up to the creature. "Come on. See, I'm not hurt. You stopped the bad men in time."

The loud snarling dimmed to a low growl.

Sergeant Wallace shoved his way through the sea of soldiers.

"What happened here?" he demanded.

"Barley showed up with his friends and decided to beat me up. The Thresl stopped them."

The ship's captain arrived in time to hear the accusation. "That's a serious charge, Lieutenant. Why would Lieutenant Barley want to attack you?" Captain Thomson asked.

"I don't know, probably because that's what he does whenever he thinks he can get away with it," Kres snapped.

"Don't listen to him!" Barley screamed. "He sicced that creature on us. I want justice." He clutched at his face with one bloody hand.

"You'll have it," the sergeant promised. Kres' heart sank in his chest. He was finally going to get the prison sentence Barley planned for him. He'd eluded it until now, but Barley wouldn't give up until Kres spent the rest of his life in a smaller cage than the Thresl.

The Thresl moved away from Barley and went to sit beside Kres. The animal sat upright, curling his tail around his body, a low purr vibrating his chest.

A group of four men wearing medic uniforms rushed over to the fallen men. They sprayed sealant on the open wounds and bound Barley's face with gauze.

"Take them to the medic ward," the captain ordered. "We'll deal with them later."

As the trio left the area, Wallace turned to the captain. "After we had a few thefts last year, I added a new camera system to the cargo hold. We can review the recording here."

Pulling a remote out of his pocket, the sergeant pressed a few buttons. Two wall panels pulled apart, revealing a large flat screen monitor.

"Now see here, Sergeant. Don't you think this should be shown in a more private location?" the captain protested.

"No. I've looked at Lieutenant Barley's record, and for some reason, all the evidence of whatever he's accused of always mysteriously disappears. I want there to be witnesses," Wallace replied.

The monitor flickered on and, after the sergeant reversed the digital recording, everyone watched as Barley attacked Kres.

Captain Thomson viewed the entire scene in silence. "After they leave the medic ward, Barley, Stanner and Philson will be confined to the brig until we reach port."

The Thresl licked his bloody claws.

Captain Thomson started shouting orders, concluding with, "Everyone clear the area except Sergeant Wallace and Lieutenant Piers."

The captain waited until everyone was gone before turning to Kres. "It seems we have a problem here, Lieutenant Piers."

"I'm so sorry, Captain Thomson," Kres said. "I really don't know why Barley hates me."

Sergeant Wallace laughed. "Probably because you're smarter, better looking, and people actually like you."

The captain smiled and slapped Sergeant Wallace on the back. "I'm so glad you recorded the incident, Wallace. I've been trying to pin something on that pompous ass since he walked onto my ship. I hate punk kids who ride on their parents' glory."

"So I'm not in trouble?" Kres asked. He couldn't believe he was getting out of this, and Barley was actually receiving the punishment he deserved. It was like a living dream.

"There is the problem of the Thresl..." Captain Thomson said.

"I didn't let him free, Captain, I promise. His cage just came open."

"I saw," the captain agreed. "But he's still imprinted on you."

Kres stared at the creature in horror. "Imprinted? No. He can't be. He's meant for an ambassador or someone." This was awful. A million-dollar Thresl imprinted on a lieutenant with little money and no pedigree. "We'll put him back in the cage. He'll be fine."

He looked down at the cat creature blinking up at him with gold eyes. "Go back into the cage, Thresl," Kres said in a soothing tone. "Go on now." He made a shooing motion with his hand. The Thresl rubbed his enormous head against Kres' stomach, a low purr rolling up from his throat.

"Yours," a voice whispered inside Kres' head.

"Oh, no, no, no. Not mine."

"Did it talk?" the captain asked curiously. "I'd heard they can sometimes mentally communicate with their bonded humans. They are an interesting breed."

"I can't have a Thresl. I can barely take care of myself," Kres objected.

"We'll have to explain to the ambassador why his present is no longer going to work." The captain gave him a smile. "I'll put that on Barley's shoulders also."

"What do I do with the Thresl?" Kres asked, bewildered.

"You'll have to be transferred to the Thresl training facility," the captain said. "It's located on the moon of their home planet of Nillre. That's the only place that conducts proper Thresl orientation. Once your training is complete, you can come back to your position as a fighting team or you can join the troops on Nillre. Since we're allies, either military group would take you. Unfortunately, you'll be useless until you've finished imprinting with the beast." The captain gave him a measuring look. "Consider yourself lucky. Not very many have the privilege of a Thresl bonding."

Kres realised it didn't matter what he wanted. Now that he'd imprinted with the Thresl, he couldn't abandon the creature that had saved his life. "Is there a shuttle I can catch?"

"Yes," Sergeant Wallace said. "I can have one ready for you in an hour if you want to get your stuff together and head for the dock."

Kres didn't have much to pack. As a soldier he was only allowed a rucksack full of clothes and a few personal items.

"Thank you, Sergeant, for all your help." He hoped he was able to convey his gratitude to the man who'd essentially saved him from prison. After saluting both officers, he turned to leave.

"Aren't you forgetting something?" Wallace asked.

The Thresl bounded after him, his huge body as tall as Kres' chest.

Kres looked back at the cage. "Do I need a collar or something?"

The Thresl gave a low growl.

Captain Thomson shook his head. "He's yours now. He won't do anything unless you are in danger, and if that is the case, you don't want to be on the other side of a leash."

The hair on Kres' arms stood on end. He could see no way this was going to end well.

Sighing, Kres headed to his room.

* * * *

The shuttle trip to the Thresl moon gave Kres plenty of time to think over the mess his life had become.

Unfortunately, no amount of analysing uncovered a secret escape plan to his current situation. Still stunned over the new path his career had taken, Kres curled up in his shuttle seat beside his purring companion and let exhaustion take over.

Someone shook his shoulder, pulling him out of his slumber. A large man in a military uniform towered over him. "Are you Kreslan Piers?"

Kres rubbed the sleep out of his eyes. "Yeah."

"I'm Jones. Come with me."

Kres blinked at the Thresl as he rubbed against him, almost knocking him off his feet. "Take it easy," he muttered as he stood up, hoping the beast didn't push him over in his rush of affection.

"Wow, that's the biggest Thresl I've ever seen," the soldier said, eyeing the beast nervously. "Where's his cage?"

Kres gave the cat beast a long look.

It purred.

"The captain said a bonded Thresl didn't need one."

The soldier gave him a shy smile. "Sorry, my information was faulty. I thought you were escorting it here. I didn't know you were the bonded one. In general, they are saved for ambassadors, kings, high-ranking officers and the occasional diplomat. I've never seen one bonded with a lieutenant. How did you get it to bond with you?" The soldier watched Kres as if he were going to confess a deep dark secret.

"Just lucky I guess." Kres glared at the creature. The Thresl jumped up, placed his paws on Kres' shoulders and licked his cheek.

"Lucky."

The word whispered through Kres' mind with a tone of smug satisfaction that made him laugh. He gently pushed the overly affectionate creature away.

"I'll escort you to the training facility. Admiral Holland is waiting to meet you. Now I know why. It's rare that a regular soldier has the acceptance of a Thresl. Everyone's going to be jealous. I suspect there will be bets going around that you'll not get it fully bonded. I'll put my money on you, so don't let me down."

"I'll try not to," Kres said. He was making no promises. If things went horribly wrong, maybe he could ditch the growly beast.

The Thresl snorted beside him. Not for the first time Kres wondered about the beast's IQ. He'd heard they were an intelligent race, but he had no idea how intelligent. He knew little about them since they weren't something he ran into every day. Rumours flew about how they changed into humans, but in the short span of time between bonding with the Thresl to being sent on the shuttle Kres had learnt nothing new.

It was a short walk from the dock to central command. Admiral Holland met them just outside his office. Jones quickly made the introductions before stepping back and trying to be as unobtrusive as possible. The admiral was a big man with cropped blond hair and an expression on his face that said he didn't accept excuses from anyone. His eyes were like chips of ice as he looked Kres over.

The Thresl didn't approve. Placing himself between Kres and Holland, the beast opened his mouth, flashed his razor sharp teeth and gave a low growl.

"Control your beast."

"You're going to get my ass kicked," Kres projected towards the Thresl.

A soft chuffing noise came from the beast. He moved back to stand at Kres' side.

"Impressive." The admiral's cold eyes held grudging approval.

Kres didn't bother telling the man he had little control over the Thresl. It was probably better at this point to let the man have his illusions. The more command others thought he had over the Thresl, the better the chance he could keep the cat free and find a good home for him in the future.

The Thresl growled at Kres.

"Hush," Kres murmured at him. He didn't want to fight with the big cat, especially not in front of the admiral.

"I am assigning you to basic training. It's to help you work as a partner with your Thresl and decide its final form."

"Is it true they turn into humans?"

"Sometimes," the admiral said. "It depends. They generally choose some sort of humanoid form, but I've seen them turn into wolfmen, three-armed bears, and even once, an octopus for a sea-dwelling bondmate. I would say over ninety per cent of the time they are some sort of human. Unfortunately, you don't get to pick its form. It will pick the shape it thinks will suit you best."

"How will training help the Thresl decide on a form?"

The admiral shrugged. "I'm not sure how it works, but something about the Thresl psyche helps it determine what would be the best fit for its master. You will learn more details in your class. For now, take your bag and drop it off in your room. You can head directly to the classroom in the south wing after that. Jones can show you where you need to go."

Kres saluted the admiral before taking his leave. *Great.* A large cat followed him around, and he was going back into military training.

He was never going to have sex again.

Chapter Two

The training area was an empty white room with three other human and Thresl pairs.

"You must be Kres." A large man with a nice collection of scars stood at the front of the room with a beautiful black-haired woman. When she turned to look at him, Kres could see from the Thresl gold eyes she wasn't human.

"I'm Commander Tiller, and this is my Thresl, Muir."

"Nice to meet you." Kres saluted the commander and gave the Thresl a polite bow.

"Why did you do that?" the commander asked.

"Do what?" Kres looked at the man in confusion.

"Bow to my Thresl."

"It's rude to not acknowledge another being." His mother had taught him good manners.

The commander looked him over as if inspecting a new life form. "I've introduced Muir to thousands of people over the years, and you are the first to acknowledge her as an individual being."

Kres found that hard to believe, but he wasn't going to call the commander a liar. However, his expression must've given him away.

"You don't believe me." The commander laughed. He turned to the other humans in the room. "Did any of you acknowledge Muir?" The other three men shook their heads, and all of them gave Kres measuring looks as if wondering how he'd fit into the group.

Great – more buddies.

Kres' Thresl stepped in front of him and let out a low growl.

The other three Thresls hid behind their humans.

"I guess we've discovered who's alpha in this pack," the commander said with satisfaction.

"What do you mean?" one of the other men asked.

"Kres, these are your training partners Davis, Zander and Brice. Together you will learn how to work with and fight alongside your Thresls. Eventually, they will transform into the perfect partner for you." He motioned to his own Thresl. "Muir is a specialist in diplomacy and small weapons, both things that have gotten me out of more than one tight spot. The shape your Thresl takes will determine where you go next in your training. When Thresls are first trained, they need an alpha – a pack leader if you will. Since Kres' Thresl is the biggest and most aggressive of the four, he will become the alpha of this group." He turned to examine Kres closely. "Has he grown since he was freed from his cage?"

Kres looked his Thresl over. "Not really. He was pretty damn big to begin with."

"Hmm. Interesting. His aggression is surprising in a Thresl not yet fully bonded."

Muir stepped forward.

"Yes, Muir?"

"I think we should start them out with the loyalty test." Her voice was silky smooth, the voice of someone who used charm to get her way. Next to the rough commander, Kres could see how they meshed together. They were a good fit. Kres didn't want to be a perfect partner with a Thresl. He wanted to be a spaceship captain, and he didn't see that happening while he had a Thresl to watch over.

"Good thinking," Commander Tiller said. "Davis, come forward."

Davis walked to the front of the room until he stood before the commander. He wore his dark hair cropped short, and the Thresl beside him had light brown fur. Davis looked quite a bit older than Kres and had an air of command.

Without warning, the Commander picked up a firearm and shot at Davis' feet. The Thresl took the back of Davis' shirt in his teeth and tugged him away from the danger.

"Good instincts," Commander Tiller said. "You may step back."

The pair went back into line.

"Brice, your turn."

Brice was a blond with long hair and an earring in one ear. Kres bet his parents had purchased his Thresl, a shiny black-furred creature more pretty than powerful.

"You're not gonna shoot me, are you, Commander?" he asked in a slow drawl.

"I might if you don't stop sleeping with my staff," the commander growled.

The commander pointed his gun at Brice, and the Thresl hid behind the human.

"Failed," Commander Tiller said.

"What do you mean failed?" Brice demanded, stomping his foot.

"I mean your parents can buy you a Thresl, but they can't make it bond with you. You've had yours for three months, and it won't lift a paw to save you when someone is holding a gun on you. No devotion. Your Thresl will be collected and given to another owner."

"No!" Brice screamed.

"This is a military base. I don't care who your father is. I'm not going to force a Thresl who isn't interested in bonding. You can try to get another or head back home."

"But I don't want it for military use!" Brice glared at the commander.

The commander didn't look impressed and Kres watched as the commander subtly pushed a button on the communicator strapped to his wrist. "A Thresl's first instinct is to protect its bonded. Your father acquired yours to be a personal bodyguard. If it doesn't want to guard you then it isn't going to be what you need. If it wanted to be your pet, it would still want to protect you. Basically, by hiding behind you, the Thresl said it would rather you were killed than it. So you failed." The commander spoke slowly as if talking to a child.

Brice glared at the Commander. "This isn't over." He turned to go. He stopped when his Thresl didn't follow. "Come!"

The cat flattened its ears and ignored the command.

Brice flushed red. He opened his mouth but before he could argue further, two soldiers in medic uniforms rushed in and herded the Thresl out of the room.

"You know the law," Commander Tiller said. "No Thresl can be kept if it refuses to bond with you."

Kres' heart slammed against his chest. *"You can still get out of this."* He hoped his telepathic message would get across.

The Thresl purred.

Brice left in a stomping fury. If there had been a door, he would've slammed it.

"Zander, you're next."

A slim man with cropped black hair and intense blue eyes stepped forward. Commander Tiller raised his gun to fire. Zander's Thresl knocked him to the ground, covering him with his own body.

"Excellent," the commander praised. "Kres, you're next."

"I don't think that is such a good idea, Commander. My Thresl doesn't like it when people aim weapons at me."

"That's the idea. Don't be a wimp. I thought you were a soldier." Commander Tiller's eyes were hard with anger.

"You were warned," Kres said. He stepped forward.

As soon as the commander pointed the gun at Kres, his Thresl leapt forward and slammed into the commander, taking him to the floor. The Thresl latched his sharp teeth onto the man's wrist. Screaming, Tiller dropped his weapon.

Satisfied the man was unarmed, Kres' Thresl released the commander's wrist but remained over him, staring with teeth bared, growling low.

"I am so fucked," Kres muttered. Muir stepped forward, but the Thresl snapped his teeth at her. She turned her head so they were no longer making eye contact.

"Thresl, come here!" Kres shouted.

With a last growl, the Thresl left his prey and walked over to Kres. He circled Kres, rubbing his body all over him, evidently making sure he was marked with his scent, before sitting on his haunches with a rumbly purr. Kres scowled at the smug expression on the beast's face.

Muir pressed the emergency button, and the two medical personnel came back into the room.

The commander was quickly bandaged and given a shot to prevent infection. Muir then helped the white-faced commander to his feet. The look he gave Kres was filled with an admiration he hadn't expected.

"That was truly impressive, and I can't say you didn't warn me." The older soldier gave a rusty chuckle. "I've had Thresls growl, cower, knock down their owners, but I've never seen one so determined to totally take out the threat and protect what was his. That is not only the biggest damn Thresl I've ever seen, he's the most devoted."

"Y-you don't think he can be re-bonded with someone else, do you?" Kres tried not to convey how much he really wanted that to be the case. He didn't want to hurt the cat's feelings, but damn, he didn't want to be here. His plans didn't include becoming a beast's pet.

The commander gave him a pitying look. "Sorry, kid, you were meant to be the bonded match of a Thresl."

Kres' Thresl gave a snarl.

"I meant a match for *that* Thresl," the commander corrected himself.

A low purr filled the air.

"I hope you didn't have plans for a wife, because most Thresls won't share." He gave a fond look at Muir. "Even the most mild-mannered Thresl."

Muir smiled, showing off a set of sharp teeth.

"No, I didn't have any plans for a wife, but I was kind of hoping for a husband." Kres gave the Thresl a sad look. The creature stood on his back legs and licked his cheek.

"Sorry, soldier, but if you're lucky, your Thresl will take that into consideration when he chooses a form.

"The first lesson for the day is over." The Commander looked at his wrist communicator. "Get some rest and we'll start something less violent tomorrow."

* * * *

The room assigned to them was the usual military barrack room with sterile white walls, a bed with a thin mattress, and minimal comforts. The only difference was the large pillow splayed out on the floor.

The Thresl walked over to the pillow, gave it a sniff then jumped onto the bed.

"No, bad cat, that's my bed."

The Thresl flattened his ears as he stared at Kres.

"No." He crossed his arms. "I am not sleeping on the floor."

Purring, the animal scooted over, leaving a Kres-sized space beside him. A satisfied expression filled the beast's gold eyes.

Sighing, Kres stripped down to his underwear and climbed between the sheets. "I might as well get used to you. It doesn't look like you're going anywhere." The purring at his back was loud, but the constant vibration and warmth soothed him. Tension from the day eased from his body. Before he had time to worry about the future, he was sound asleep.

The Thresl curled next to his human, sniffing at the young man he'd chosen as his. He smelt sweet. The Thresl wanted to roll around in the man's essence until he stank of the soldier's scent. He had to stay close. He didn't trust the other soldiers. They looked at his man like they wanted to do him harm.

No one was allowed to hurt his man.

His.

Growling gently, the creature slid closer, curling his body around the human. A crackling sound filled the air as his bones adjusted to their new larger form. He needed to be bigger and stronger than the others. None of them could threaten what was his.

Pain ripped through his frame as his body elongated and his muscles expanded to realign to a new body shape. He could feel his heartbeat thrum as his blood increased its flow through his veins to feed his growth.

Fully focused on the sleeping man beside him, the Thresl concentrated. It was his nature to become the perfect counterpart to his bondmate. Kres was a handsome, intelligent man with a good heart and strong ethics, a man who needed someone to watch his back. To let others know he wasn't prey.

The Thresl bit his lips to keep back a shout. He didn't want to wake Kres and disturb him with his transformation. His entire body burned as hair sank into smooth tanned skin, his claws retracted, and his spine snapped into its final formation. Once the change was complete, he would abandon his cat form forever.

He would miss his tail.

A whimper escaped the Thresl, making Kres stir uneasily in the bunk beside him.

"Shh. Shh," he whispered through the pain. His sweet man didn't need to see this. To outsiders, the transformation was a horror to observe. Unfortunately, the change came when it willed, and he hadn't had a chance to get away before the transformation hit. He desperately sent out a sleeping scent to keep his human unconscious.

After what felt like hours, the Thresl gave in to the pain and fell asleep.

Chapter Three

Kres stirred in his sleep. Something was off, disturbing his rest. Shifting his position didn't work because he was held too tightly.

Held?

Blinking awake, he cautiously turned to look over his shoulder. Letting out a shout, he startled his bedmate into letting him go and tumbled out of bed.

Kres didn't even feel his ass hit the floor. His eyes were too focused on the person in his bed. The man was well over six feet tall, edging closer to seven since his feet hung off the bed. Despite feeling like a voyeur, he crawled towards the bed to examine the man more closely. Light brown skin covered a body formed with hard muscle and long limbs.

Dark brown hair grew in a short mass on the top of his head. Kres longed to plunge his fingers into the man's locks and sample the flavour of the stranger's lush lips. Glancing up, he felt a shock as familiar gold eyes looked back at him.

Thresl.

"Morning, Kres." The low gravelly voice sent shivers up Kres' spine and caused goosebumps to spread across his skin.

"Morning, Thresl."

The Thresl's lush mouth quirked up on one side. The sight sent heated images into Kres' mind about nibbling on those full lips.

"You must assign me a name," the Thresl said with an inviting smile. "As I have shifted, now we are bound."

Shit.

Kres felt guilty about lusting after the gorgeous shifter when it was his fault the creature had changed at all. There had to be a specialist who could help get the Thresl back to his original form. Despite his attraction to the gorgeous creature, he knew if he touched the Thresl, there was no hope for escape. He'd be bound to another being for the rest of his life. When the commander had said the Thresl would become his perfect partner, Kres had thought he meant fighting partner, but the shifter's appearance put that assumption into question. No one could've looked more like the type of man whom Kres was attracted to than the male on the bed.

Gold eyes watched him carefully as if searching his expression for something. Kres averted his gaze. He hoped the man-cat couldn't sense his lust. He didn't know how deep their connection went at this point, but he wouldn't force himself on the sexy creature.

"What name do you want?"

Kres struggled to carry on the conversation, focusing on the floor instead of the tempting naked man splayed out on his bed.

"*You* have to pick it."

Reluctantly, Kres looked into the Thresl's eyes. The understanding there almost broke him.

"I-I can't," Kres forced out through his quickly closing throat as panic sped up his heart.

"We can't go back to before. I can't unpick you," the Thresl said in a gentle tone as if afraid of further freaking Kres out.

"Why did you pick me to start with?" It was a question he'd obsessed over since the cat had first chosen him.

The Thresl tilted his head, the gesture a shadow of the feline he had once been. "I chose you because I could choose no other. You were the one."

He sounded so definite that Kres didn't know what to say. How could he explain he didn't feel the same way? It was like giving the speech to a guy—*it's not you, it's me*—except in this case there was no way to break up. He was stuck with this gorgeous man-cat forever. His nebulous plans of finding a good man to settle down with while he rose in the military ranks vanished. He'd left his home to carve his own path in life, only to have it chosen for him. He remembered his grandfather's favourite saying—*'You don't choose your fate, your fate chooses you.'* As usual, his grandfather was right.

"Name me," the Thresl insisted.

Kres wrapped his arms around himself. If he named the Thresl, it would make it too real. It was the point of no return. It was like naming the stray cat that followed you home. Once it was named, you couldn't just dump it at the animal shelter.

He wondered, slightly hysterically, if there was a Thresl drop-off shelter to return lost or unwanted shape-shifters.

"I-I can't." The sad look in the Thresl's eyes shook Kres, but he had to stay strong.

"You still hope to leave me." The Thresl's resigned tone stabbed Kres with guilt.

"I hope to free you," Kres corrected. He knew he was battling against the tide but it wasn't his nature to go down without a fight.

The Thresl laughed. "Thresls aren't meant to be free. We're meant to be bonded. There's no greater shame than to remain in our birth form until death. I am young for my kind and will have high status for my early transformation."

He looked so proud of himself Kres couldn't continue his denial. For the Thresl, this was a lifetime milestone to be proud of and celebrated. For Kres, it was a life-changing event—and not a particularly welcome one. Looking over the tall muscular man in his bed, he had to admit there could be worse ways to spend his life than in the presence of a sexy man dedicated to being his.

"Name me!" the Thresl insisted again.

While Kres was thinking about how his life was taking a horribly wrong turn, his new life partner was fixated on his name. Kres wished there was a way to give the Thresl his freedom, but apparently that wish wasn't shared by the ex-cat. Taking a deep breath, Kres accepted his fate.

Kres cautiously held out his hands. The Thresl gave him a wide smile and wrapped his larger hands around Kres'.

Kres looked at the gorgeous dark-haired man and thought over various names. There were a lot of names that could suit his new companion. Tristan? Litger? Neel? A forgotten memory drifted into his mind. *Perfect.*

"When I was little, my mother used to read to me every night. My favourite story was about a beast that terrorised the local villagers until he met a fair maiden. He fell in love with her and shed his animal skin to stay a human at her side." Kres could feel a blush heat his cheeks as the Thresl's smile widened. "I know this isn't the same situation, but I've always liked the name of the hero. His name was Vohne."

The Thresl released Kres' hands and slid them into his hair. Using a firm grip, he pulled Kres closer until their mouths met in a slow, demanding kiss. Heat poured through Kres' body like molten lava, burning him throughout. A moan rolled from his chest, vibrating their lips and adding to the sensation. When he was finally released, he had to blink a bit to focus his vision.

"The situation isn't that different," the Thresl said before nipping at Kres' bottom lip. "I'd be happy to take the name of Vohne."

A loud banging shook Kres out of his daze.

Someone was at the door.

A low growl rolled from Vohne's throat. He jumped off the bed into a protective crouch. He quickly straightened, stomped to the door then ripped it open.

It took Kres an inhuman amount of effort to tear his eyes from the Thresl's tight, naked ass when he heard his name.

"Piers!" Commander Tiller's voice crackled with command.

He rushed to the door to see the commander's eyes wide with fear as he took in the enormous man at the door.

"You might want to tell your boyfriend I'm not a threat."

"Um, that's not my boyfriend – that's my Thresl."

"My name is Vohne. Kres has gifted me with a name." The Thresl sounded ridiculously proud of that fact.

Tiller shifted his gaze from the huge man to Kres. "Report to my office ASAP."

With those words, Commander Tiller turned and marched away. Kres grabbed the Thresl by the arm and pulled him back into the room, closing the door behind them. Although soldiers were generally difficult to shock, he didn't want to get complaints about a naked man hanging out in his doorway. He didn't need that on his permanent record.

Running a hand through his rumpled hair, he thought through his options.

"I'm going to take a shower, then I'm going to have to go to the commissary and buy you some clothes."

"I will go with you," the Thresl announced.

"You can't go with me. You're naked."

Vohne crossed his arms over his chest. "Then you can't go. I can't protect you if you go by yourself."

Kres laughed. "You don't need to protect me. I'm just going to the store."

"You don't go anywhere I don't go." His tone was so definite, Kres knew he wasn't going to get out of it. Maybe in time the creature would become less possessive.

"I'm going to take a shower. We will discuss this when I'm done."

Vohne took a step to follow, but Kres pointed at the bed. "Stay. If anyone jumps out to attack me under the hot water spray, I'll give a shout."

Fuming, Kres stomped to the bathroom, making sure to slam the door when he entered. He quickly felt foolish. In an unfamiliar environment, the Thresl was just sticking with what he knew—protect his human above all other things. Strange none of the other Thresls appeared as protective of their matches as Vohne was of him.

Still thinking over his odd relationship, Kres turned on the water and sighed beneath the hot stream. Slowly his muscles relaxed until his stress rinsed down the drain.

Maybe he could call someone and have some clothes delivered. Pleased with the new plan, Kres finished up his shower and pulled open the curtain.

"Ahhh!" Clutching his chest, he glared at the large man who had invaded the bathing space. "You scared me."

Vohne looked at him with concern. "You are injured?" He reached for Kres, who stepped back from his touch. "You are afraid of me?"

"I'm afraid of anyone who appears in the bathroom while I'm washing. I wasn't expecting you."

Vohne looked Kres up and down. A wide smile crossed his face. "You should expect others if you are going to walk around wet and naked. You are very pleasing to the eyes. I am honoured to call you mine."

"I-I... Never mind."

He didn't have it in him to tell Vohne that he didn't belong to the shifter. They both knew there was a bond between them. He just wasn't sure what that meant in the long term.

"It is a waste to wrap clothes around you. The only reason I will allow it is because I've observed that your kind doesn't walk around naked due to your fragile skins."

"You have a fragile skin now also," Kres reminded him.

He got an indecent smile in return. "Maybe we should see what happens when you rub the two of us together."

A knock at the outer door had them both turning.

Kres wrapped a towel around his hips. "There sure is a lot of traffic this early in the morning."

Before he could reach the main living area, Vohne raced past him and ripped open the door.

A messenger stood there holding out a package. "The commander said you might need this."

Kres shoved Vohne to the side, pushing his way past him. "I'll take that. Tell the commander thank you."

The messenger looked Kres up and down in appreciation. "Let me know if there is anything else I can do for you."

Vohne let out a growl and yanked Kres back into the room. "Get your own human." With a snarl, he slammed the door in the messenger's face.

"Nice." Kres folded his arms and glared at the Thresl. "If you're going to pretend to be human, you have to learn to have better manners."

Vohne narrowed his golden eyes. "Why would I want to do that?"

"So people don't give in to the urge to shoot you with their side arms."

"Not that." Vohne waved a hand as if swatting away a pesky fly. "Why would I want to pretend to be human? I am a Thresl. I am not human and never will be. Despite my form, I will always be a beast inside." The creature gave Kres a toothy smile. "Don't worry so much about what other people think."

With that sage advice, the creature walked past Kres into the bathroom, leaving the door open behind him.

"I am in so much trouble," Kres groaned and rubbed his face with his hands. Forcing his eyes away from the bathroom, he finished dressing, making sure his uniform was tidy and his boots had a nice shine. He was certain that by the end of the day he'd need as many extra points as he could get with his commander. The stress he'd lost in the shower came back with a vengeance. Grumbling about naked, sexy Thresls, Kres opened the package the messenger had brought, pulled out the clothes, and laid them out for the man-cat to find when he got out of the shower.

* * * *

Commander Tiller sat behind his desk as he regarded them with his cool grey eyes. His beautiful Thresl, Muir, gave them a nod as they entered. Kres nodded back. Vohne gave a low growl. Muir tilted her head in acknowledgement of his alpha status.

Kres resisted the urge to roll his eyes since Tiller was watching him, but it was close. It would take some time to get used to the pecking order of Thresls. They appeared to take it seriously if Muir's behaviour was any indication.

"Please be seated," Tiller indicated the chairs set before his desk.

Kres settled in the chair on the left. He wasn't surprised when Vohne stood behind him instead of taking a seat. Sitting would be too laid back for the Thresl. After all, how was he going to protect Kres from all those imaginary dangers if he relaxed enough to sit down?

"Piers, I'm not going to tiptoe around the problem. Your Thresl is dangerous. I've never seen one transform that quickly before. The faster they transform, the more powerful the Thresl." His cool eyes looked Vohne over from head to toe. "I've also never seen one so big. There are a lot of people who are going to want your Thresl."

"B-but I thought now that we were bonded we had to stay together?" He didn't want to sound like a whiny child, but he was just now getting used to the idea of having this large creature follow him around.

"That's why they will try to grab you, too. Your Thresl will do anything if they have you under their control."

Kres took a deep breath. "Won't Vohne just kill them?"

Tiller gave him a disapproving look. "You really don't know much about the Thresl, do you?"

"What he doesn't know I can teach him," Vohne growled behind him.

The commander looked them both over. Sighing, he reached into his desk and pulled out a thick book. He slammed it onto his desk. "Take this and look it over. It should tell you everything you need to know about bonding with a Thresl, but don't think just because you're bonded no one can use him."

Kres frowned. "What would they use him for?"

Tiller looked Vohne up and down. "Yours they would use as an assassin. Thresls are excellent killers, especially if they're trying to get their mate back. Even if they don't have you, the promise of reuniting the two of you will keep him under their control for a while.

"It is your job to protect him as much as he protects you. I'm putting the pair of you on a special training task force. You will have limited contact with other people until your bond is secure. The stronger the bond, the better you'll be able to sense each other if you get separated. Understand?"

"I thought we were already bonded," Kres said.

Tiller smiled. "Read the book. It'll explain everything. Dismissed."

Kres picked up the heavy volume, more than certain the complicated question of his feelings for the man-cat wouldn't be answered inside.

Kres took the Thresl to the cafeteria. He couldn't help looking at everyone he passed with suspicion. It disturbed him to learn that someone could still try to steal his Thresl or kidnap him to control Vohne. Possessiveness sat oddly in his chest when he looked at the man-cat. He still wasn't quite sure what to do with the creature, but he certainly didn't want anyone else taking him either.

"It will be all right." Vohne rubbed a reassuring hand down Kres' back.

He almost dropped the book.

"Um, thanks. I...I just thought once you were bonded, you were safe from poachers. I mean, I'm sorry you didn't get to your destination, but I don't want you stolen either."

Vohne gave him a wide smile, exposing all of his extra sharp teeth. "I'm hoping someone tries. Then they can learn the Thresl truth."

"What's that?" Kres was positive there was more going on in this conversation than appeared on the surface, and he was almost as certain he didn't want to learn what it was.

"Kres!" Zander ran up to him like he was his new best friend. Vohne gave an unfriendly growl.

"Hi, Zander." He saw Zander's Thresl plodding behind him. The animal was caramel-coloured and several shades lighter than Vohne had been in that form. He gave a friendly smile to the creature, but its eyes were focused on Vohne. The creature tilted its head submissively. With a satisfied nod, Vohne turned his attention to Zander.

"Wow, I heard your Thresl converted early, but shit, he's big."

The awe in Zander's voice made Kres laugh. He liked Zander and hoped they could become friends.

"Hey, did you hear what happened with Brice?"

Kres leant forward as the other man lowered his voice. "He was arrested and thrown in the brig. He tried to steal back that Thresl he'd bought even after the commander said they weren't a match."

A chill went down Kres' spine. Brice reminded him a lot of Barley. Maybe there was a law—if your name started with a B, you had to be a total asshole. Kres quickly reviewed the people he knew whose name started with B and decided it was just a fluke.

"How did he get caught?"

"The Thresl bit him. When he started screaming, the MPs came and discovered he was trying to steal the Thresl. It's a felony, but his rich father will probably get him off."

"Probably." Kres bitterly reflected from his own experience that that was usually the case.

"What's the next step in your training?" Zander asked, regarding the pair.

"We're supposed to bond." He waved his book at Zander. "The commander gave me this to review."

"Huh." Zander looked at the book curiously. "I wonder if there are diagrams."

"What are you talking about?"

Zander gave him a wide smile, his electric blue eyes lighting up with laughter. "There's only one way to truly bond with a Thresl."

Kres had a bad feeling he already knew what it was. The hand settling on his lower back reinforced the feeling. It stroked temptingly close to his ass as Zander spoke.

"You have to have sex." Zander looked the Thresl up and down. "Maybe a lot of sex."

"Crap," Kres muttered.

Vohne let out a low rumble behind him. Apparently converting to human hadn't removed his ability to purr.

Kres gave an involuntary shudder. The thought of being intimate with the gorgeous creature behind him overwhelmed his senses. What the hell had he got into? He'd gone from thinking he'd never have sex again to discovering it was a requirement for the safety of the being that had already claimed him. This entire bonding situation was taking over his life. How had he gone from a simple soldier with an eye on becoming a captain to the other half of a killing machine? A sigh passed his lips as Kres realised how truly different his future would now be.

Vohne stroked a hand up and down Kres' back.

"Why don't you join us for lunch? I was going to get a plate and sit over there." Zander pointed to an empty table in the corner of the room.

"Go sit. I will get you sustenance," Vohne offered.

"Are you sure?" Kres wasn't certain he wanted to chance letting Vohne get his food, but the look he got said the Thresl wanted to do this for him.

"Go." Vohne gave him a little nudge.

Kres shrugged and went to sit down.

Vohne turned to the other human and glared. "I was trying to break it to him gently."

"That's because you don't know anything about that kind of human. I've only known Kres for a little while, but I can already tell he's the type of person it's best to tell everything at once. Once the shock wears off, he'll make a plan to cope. If you give him things in bits and pieces, it gives him time to panic. He's a soldier. He's used to dealing with the unexpected."

"Hmm." Zander did make sense. "I will take your advice and not harm you after all." Vohne smiled, letting the human see the sharpness of his teeth. He might not have his tail anymore, but he didn't want the other man to confuse him with a human either.

"I understand that my human will need some friends, and it will benefit him to know someone who also has a Thresl. However, if you harm him, I will have to kill you." He made sure his look said he wasn't kidding. Vohne wanted Zander to know he took his responsibility seriously.

"Um, okay." Zander gave him a weak smile. "Will my Thresl be like you?"

Vohne laughed. "You humans still don't get it, do you?"

Zander shook his head. "Don't get what?"

"How Thresls choose their form."

"No one understands that," Zander argued.

Vohne had to admire how Zander rallied after Vohne's intimidation. He would be a valuable friend for his mate.

"Thresls understand." Vohne looked over at his human, who was watching him with a worried expression in his eyes. "Thresls become the essence of the person they bond with."

"So the commander is, deep down, a female diplomat?"

Vohne nodded. "He probably appreciates art and music but was told when he was young it wasn't manly enough to pursue those interests."

"And Kres? Deep inside he's an almost seven foot man with violent tendencies?"

"Yes." Vohne smirked. "Deep down, my mate is a soldier who can snap your neck if you bother him too much. But don't worry. He never will."

Zander dared to look the Thresl in the eyes. "Why is that?"

"Because I would do it for him."

Pleased he'd made his point, Vohne went to get his human some food. He didn't tell Zander that as he evolved he would lose some of his more violent urges and Kres would gain more aggression. They would find a balance until they were so close their minds would almost be as one while their bodies would feel the urge to join. The magic of Thresl-human bonding was they would both become stronger. He also didn't share what being an alpha really meant.

He would share that information only with his mate.

Chapter Four

Kres didn't know what Zander and Vohne had discussed while grabbing food, but his fellow classmate was giving him a cautious glance from time to time, as if he worried Kres was going to jump across the table and attack him.

"Is there a problem?" Kres asked before popping another piece of meat into his mouth. All morning he'd had an odd craving for red meat. Since he was usually a borderline vegetarian, it was extremely strange—but then, what *hadn't* been weird lately? The fact that Vohne had known he needed meat and had brought him a giant platter also needed further investigation, but he'd do it later when he wasn't shoving beef down his throat as fast as he could.

"Um, no?" The answer was more of a question than a statement of fact.

"What did you say to him?" he asked the Thresl.

Vohne shrugged. "I told him where the Thresl form comes from."

He could see getting a straight answer would be like yanking out one of the Thresl's fangs—difficult and potentially painful.

Taking another bite of food, he gave Zander a curious look, silently prompting the other man to continue.

"He is your inner form," Zander said.

Kres choked. He was saved from a blocked airway by a pat on the back from Vohne that nearly broke his spine.

"You are *my* inner form?"

The Thresl smiled, exposing full fangs. "Surprise."

Kres looked the large man up and down. "I must have a great inner warrior thing going on."

"Yes, you do."

He was unsettled by the serious expression in Vohne's eyes. A loud explosion startled him out of their locked gaze.

Billowy, black smoke filled the cafeteria as smoke bombs detonated in the doorway. Kres tensed, wishing he hadn't left his weapon in his room, but he hadn't expected a synchronised attack over a steak dinner. He saw Vohne's eyes glow in the dim light. A large hand clamped over his wrist and pulled him farther into the room, away from the invading smoke.

"They've come for us," Vohne said.

"Whoever they are, they can't have you." There were many things Kres was uncertain about in their relationship, but there was no way he was going to let some Thresl-kidnapping bastards take his Vohne. Kres held his breath against the smoke as the room was entirely darkened by the bombs.

Blinding lights cut through the blackness as at least a dozen men entered wearing masks and carrying weapons with light scopes.

Vohne dropped to the ground, pulling Kres with him. "Whatever happens, don't let them take you. I will always return. Remember that."

"What?" Kres gasped. He tried to figure what was going on as a loud roar filled the room, and the air closest to him was displaced by Vohne's departure as the Thresl ran directly into the blackness.

Choking on the smoke, Kres tried to stay as still as possible as screams echoed about him. He wondered where Zander was and if they had captured Zander's Thresl. He still wasn't sure what the soldiers were doing there, but he had a bad feeling. He agreed with Vohne that they were there for the Thresls. If they could catch the valuable cats, they could rake in a fortune on the black market with the ones that hadn't bonded yet. He wondered how they had got past security. Someone was going to be court-martialled for letting the invaders in.

From what he'd overheard on the shuttle to the moon, they were on a secret facility. Someone, somewhere had said too much, and now Kres was going to lose his man-cat before they'd even completed their bond. A weapon rattled as it hit the ground beside him.

Kres snatched it up, quickly familiarising himself with the controls. He might not have his Thresl's massive size, but he wasn't a weak, quivering soul to cower under the table and let someone else fight his battles.

Carefully feeling along until he had a wall to his back, Kres stalked the men who had dared to come and try to take what was his.

A sharp shout had him stepping back in time to avoid the body falling to the floor. Without a second thought, he relieved the dead man of the knife strapped to his thigh and tucked it into the back of his waistband.

He still couldn't see more than a few inches in front of him. The smoke bombs were the high quality kind that created a lot of smoke and kept it in the air. Staying perfectly still, he tried to hear any signs of Vohne nearby. He silently cursed their lack of bonding. If he'd got over his trepidation with the Thresl, they'd already have a link and he wouldn't be blindly searching for the man-cat. When he found Vohne, he was going to make sure they bonded so well he'd be able to sense him in a Zevan mud storm during swelling season.

A sudden silence filled the room, more chilling than the screams and fire-fight of moments before. Kres dared to breathe, but only in quick silent gasps. However, his heart was knocking so hard against his chest he was worried the sound alone would give him away.

"I got him!" A strong arm was wrapped around his throat. "Drop the gun," the man growled in his ear.

Kres was surprised at the lack of fear he felt as his weapon clattered to the floor. Being held by the enemy, he expected to feel something other than the complete and utter calm that took over his mind. As the stranger tried to choke the life out of him, Kres slipped his hand between them, grabbed the handle of the knife out of the back of his pants, and with ruthless precision plunged the knife into his enemy's stomach.

Howling, the man released him. For a moment it felt like the world was moving in slow motion as Kres scooped up the dropped weapon then fired it into the forehead of the other man. With a dispassionate eye, he watched the soldier drop to the ground.

"Remind me not to piss you off," Zander whispered beside him.

Kres spun around to see his new friend crouched along the wall. Still wrapped in the odd calm, Kres replied, "I don't think you'll need a reminder."

Zander's Thresl meowed imperiously.

"My Thresl says they took Vohne down the hallway."

"You can understand him?"

Zander gave him an odd look. "You couldn't understand Vohne?"

Kres shrugged. "A few words while he was a cat but not sentences. We weren't together for very long in his cat form." Impatient with their conversation while his Thresl was being taken, he scooped up another soldier's weapon and handed it over to a bewildered Zander.

"What's this for?" Zander asked with wide eyes.

"To shoot people."

"But I've never shot anyone before." Kres could hear the fear in Zander's voice.

"You aren't a soldier?"

"I'm a diplomat."

"Well, get your diplomatic ass in gear. If they get Vohne off this station because I was chatting with you, I'll shoot you myself." He crammed the weapon into Zander's hands and headed towards the exit.

"He was right, you know," Zander babbled as he scurried after Kres.

"Right about what?" Not that he really cared. Kres' eyes were busy scanning the area for possible enemies to give the other man much attention.

"You really are a kickass warrior."

"Then let's go kick some ass." He was willing to do a lot more than that if it got his Thresl back. The bastards better have made their peace with whatever deities they worshipped, because if they resisted returning Kres' Thresl, they were going to go visit them in person. He might have hesitated to claim Vohne before, but the utter fear he'd felt when he'd watched the Thresl disappear into the smoke told him they needed to be together, if only to see how far this bonding would go.

Kres kept his weapon close to his chest as he peeked around the corner. There was no one in the halls. The bastards were ahead of them. Zander rushed over to a numeric pad on the wall. Kres watched him press a series of buttons.

"Lock down commencing," the robotic female voice announced.

"Nice!" Kres approved.

Zander shrugged. "They told us the code during training. You haven't gotten that far yet. I hope they haven't escaped." Zander tucked himself close to the wall beside Kres and scanned the area with his brilliant blue eyes. The man might not be a soldier, but he had good instincts. His Thresl stood beside him, its gold eyes gleaming with anger. The cat wasn't taking the abduction of one of its kind well.

"Can you feel him?" Zander asked.

"No." For a moment despair threatened to drown Kres, but he shoved it aside. This was no time to feel sorry for himself. He had to get his Thresl back.

"You should've bonded with him," Zander scolded.

"Shut up!" Kres snapped. He didn't need a lecture on something he already knew.

A roar had them turning to the corridor on the right. As quickly and silently as he could, Kres rushed down the hall, only pausing when he reached an intersection. The noise became louder. Someone was getting an education in the abduction of Thresls, and it wasn't going well for them.

Kres let a slow smile cross his lips.

"Don't hurt him," a male voice said. "He's no good to us if he's dead."

He wasn't going to be good for them at all.

There were only three men left. Two of them carried Vohne between them while the third ordered and cursed.

Kres didn't know if the others had gone ahead or if their bodies were left on the floor in the smoke-filled cafeteria. All he knew was that they weren't there and he wasn't going to let these three idiots take off with his man.

Leaning around the corner, he aimed his weapon at the only one not holding his Thresl. The man went down with a shot to the back of his neck.

Kres hid behind the wall as the other two men shouted.

"We've got to get out of here."

"The door's locked."

Kres smiled. The bastards were trapped.

The sound of booted feet thundered behind him.

"What's going on?" The commander's voice was hushed behind him.

"There are two of them left. They have Vohne."

"Leave one of them alive for questioning. I want to find out how they got in here," the commander ordered.

"I'll try." Kres refused to make any promises. If the choice came between keeping one alive and saving his Thresl, there wasn't any question.

"You'd better open this door," one of the abductors shouted. "If you don't, your Thresl is history."

"Let go of the Thresl and we'll let you leave," the commander responded.

"I don't believe you," the abductor shouted back.

"He's smarter than he looks," Kres muttered.

Fear almost stopped his heart. The creature that had at first seemed like an interruption to his well-planned life now was the most important thing in it. What would he do if Vohne were killed?

Vohne's voice whispered in his head, *"Mate."*

"Vohne."

"Shoot the bastard."

Without hesitation, Kres did as his Thresl had requested. Whipping around the corner, he shot the idiot threatening Vohne. A cry ripped the air as the remaining man holding Vohne tumbled to the ground beneath his weight.

Soldiers filled the hall, lifting Vohne and clearing the area of the two dead men and the one still alive. Medics arrived soon after with a gurney to take Vohne away. Kres fought through the crowd to get to Vohne's side. He had to make sure his man-cat was unhurt.

He shouted and pushed until he stood beside the gurney holding his mate. Foggy gold eyes blinked up at him. Whatever drugs they'd pumped into Vohne's body made him sluggish and uncoordinated.

Vohne gripped Kres' arm like a vice. "You did good, my warrior. I am pleased to rule with you at my side."

"To what?"

Before he could get any answers, the Thresl closed his eyes and the medics carried him away.

Zander patted him on the back. "What was he talking to you about? You're looking pale. I thought you'd be happy you have your Thresl back."

"I thought I would be too." Now he was wondering what he'd got himself into…again.

Chapter Five

Kres was told to stay away from the infirmary while the Thresl healed. Apparently alpha Thresls didn't like their mates to see them injured. Something to do with wanting to always appear strong in front of their chosen ones or some such crap. Kres hadn't really paid attention past the request for him not to go with the medics. He was more interested in hunting down his Thresl book. He didn't bother to fight his banishment from the medic ward. An argument was certain to be in their near future, and he wanted to make sure he had all the facts before it began.

As much as he cared how Vohne was doing, the man-cat looked more drugged than injured, and Kres had an objective to fulfil.

"Where are you going?" Zander asked, bouncing down the hallway behind him. If there was one thing that screamed Zander wasn't a soldier, it was the way he walked. Soldiers didn't bounce. However, despite their differences, Kres still liked him. Zander was one of those people everyone liked. Kres thought he'd do very well in the diplomatic corps.

Amber Kell

"I'm going to find that damned book."

"Why?"

"Didn't you hear him? I'm supposed to rule by his side."

"Well, yeah."

Kres spun around, pinning Zander with his stare. "You knew about this?"

Zander held up his hands in self-defence. "You really don't know anything, do you?"

"How many times do I have to tell everyone that I didn't plan for a Thresl? I wasn't supposed to get one. I didn't do any planning or training or anything. All I did was stop him from killing an idiot, and we bonded."

A smile crossed Zander's face. "You don't even know what you have. Come back to my room. I can tell you everything you need to know. Besides, I've got the good brandy. It's one advantage of growing up in a diplomatic family. You know where to procure the fine liquor."

"Deal." It would probably be easier for Zander to explain it anyway. Kres wasn't book smart. Give him a weapon and some action and he could take care of himself, but words always looked jumbled on a page when he tried to focus, and when he finally got them together to form a sentence, they inevitably didn't make any sense. He'd barely scraped by his studies with the help of a good tutor. Luckily, his combat skills balanced it all out.

Zander's room was a far cry from the sterile cube that comprised Kres' lodging. Thick rugs covered the floor, the walls were tinted a soft blue and the furnishings screamed money. It was also three times the size of Kres' room. Zander gave a self-deprecating shrug. "Did I mention my father is best friends with the station master?"

"It must be good to have connections," Kres commented.

Zander smiled. "That's what the diplomatic corps is all about. Now, come sit down." He pointed towards a well-padded chair by a table that looked like honest-to-god real wood.

Ignoring Kres' stare, Zander grabbed two crystal glasses and a full decanter. He filled one glass halfway and the other almost to the top. He slid the full one towards Kres.

"You might need this while I describe how it is going to go with you and the Thresl who will be king."

Kres felt his heart stop.

"What?"

"When the commander told you your Thresl was an alpha, he didn't tell you the entire story." He motioned to the glass of brandy. "Drink up."

Kres took a tentative sip. The liquor burned all the way down to his toes, filling his body with warmth and a tingling sensation. "Wow." A few sips later he decided he really liked the feeling. Halfway through the glass he set it down. "Now that you have me feeling good, what are you trying to not tell me?"

Zander gave him a sheepish look. "Obviously I need to work on my poker face if I'm going to make it as a politician. Here's the gist of it. True alpha Thresls are extremely rare. One hasn't been born in over a hundred years. It's one thing to be alpha of our class but another to be a real alpha Thresl. Vohne is the latter. An alpha is priceless to Thresl hunters, which is why there was an attack on the station. To control Vohne is to control the entire kingdom of Thresls.

They would've come and gotten you next so they could blackmail him into doing whatever they wanted."

Kres brushed off concern for himself. He needed to figure out what the hell was going on. "But why are they so special?"

"Because they are the strongest of their kind. Thresls are shape-shifters who can bond so well with their mates that they essentially enhance the other person. When you went after those guys earlier, how did you feel?"

Kres rolled the memory around in his mind before he answered. "Strong. Powerful. I don't remember ever feeling like that before, like I could take on anyone."

"That is your Thresl effect." Zander took a sip of the liquor before speaking. "Thresls don't just become the very heart of their owner, they strengthen them. Alphas are the kings of Thresl kind. Vohne is obligated to go back to the Thresl home planet and take his seat on the throne. He will be making decisions for the fate of his kingdom. If he says a planet isn't granted a Thresl from his people, they won't be. Thresls are the most desired commodity anywhere, and Vohne will have total control. He is also the only creature who can dissolve a Thresl bond."

"I thought they couldn't be broken." This entire bonding thing bothered Kres. He didn't like things being taken out of his hands.

"They couldn't before. The last Thresl alpha died a hundred years ago. Only the alpha is born with the ability to break connections. You didn't just bond with a strong creature that can make you a better soldier. You bonded with the king of Thresls. You are now, in essence, one of the most powerful men in the entire galaxy, my friend. And until another alpha is born, your Thresl is the king of an entire planet."

Kres grabbed his glass of liquor and downed the rest of the contents in one final gulp. He'd thought his life was screwed before. Now what was he going to do?

* * * *

Kres was lying on the bed when Vohne returned to their room. He examined every inch of his human, checking for injuries. He'd yearned for Kres while in his drug-induced haze. Everything he had longed to merge with this man but he hadn't wanted Kres to see him injured. A Thresl always wanted to appear strong and able to take care of his mate.

The look he got in return was less than promising.

"Aren't you happy to see me?"

Kres flipped a page in a book Vohne recognised as the one the commander had given his mate. "Thrilled, Your Highness." He flipped another page.

Uh-oh.

Kres definitely didn't look pleased. Obviously someone had filled him in on who Vohne must be.

Vohne decided it was best not to let his mate think too much on it. Marching over to the bed, he slid his fingers through Kres' hair and tilted his chin. "I'm happy to see you too." Without giving his mate a chance to answer, Vohne dropped to his knees on the floor and covered Kres' mouth with his own. Heat poured through him at the mouth-to-mouth connection, and all the fine hairs across his body stood on end at the electric jolt of kissing his mate.

Yum!

He might not still have his tail, but his claws were just beneath the surface. With a low growl, he shredded his mate's shirt.

"Hey!"

Kres' outraged expression didn't match the smell of passion rolling off his body.

"You wish to stop?" Vohne pressed his body closer to his mate's, rubbing against him in the most delightful way. A purr rolled up his throat.

"Um, no." Kres lifted his hips in a silent invitation to explore, an invitation Vohne was more than willing to accept. "Besides, you can unbind us if you want, right?"

Vohne froze. "What do you mean?" He didn't like the way this conversation was going. Kres didn't need to consider whether his mating could be unbound. They belonged together.

"Zander said kings can break Thresl bonds. You could unbind us if you needed to, couldn't you?"

"No." He made sure his tone left no room for doubt. He wasn't going to give his human even a smidgen of hope that Kres could ever get away from their bond. "Once we bond, you will be mine forever."

Kres tried to move away from under Vohne's touch, but there was no place he could go with Vohne pinning him to the thin mattress. "Maybe we should wait. Make sure we're compatible before we seal our fate."

Vohne couldn't stop the predatory smile he could feel crossing his face. "It was too late for you, gorgeous, when I first caught your scent. You are mine, and whether we have sex or not, you will always be mine." He kissed Kres until he felt the fit, muscular body relax beneath him. Making sure he had a good hold on his mate, he said the words that sealed the first step of the final bonding process. "I, Vohne, named by my mate, Kreslan Piers, forever pledge my heart and body to protect and cherish the man who will be mine."

He let out a sigh of relief as he felt the mating bonds twine between them like invisible strings, twisting their souls together until he couldn't tell where one started and the other ended.

"What the hell was that?" Kres jerked beneath him, reminding Vohne that the man still wore pants.

"That was our bonding. We are now mated," Vohne declared with satisfaction.

"Wait! I thought we had to have sex."

Vohne smiled. "Don't worry. That is only the first step. The rest are much more enjoyable."

Kres' throat convulsed. "How many steps are there?"

Vohne rubbed his nose against his mate's in a Thresl sign of affection. "There can be as many as we want. After all, we are kings."

Before his human could come up with any more excuses, Vohne used his claws to take care of those pesky trousers. He'd have to make sure to alert the castle staff they would need clothing stashed in every room. It felt good to be in a body again. He wondered how long he should wait to tell his nervous mate the truth about them.

This was always the fun part, getting to know his mate in each new incarnation. Two thousand years of being born, hunting down his mate and eventually dying, and he still found it exciting each time. It was too bad his mate never remembered his former lives. Of course, that always made the courtship that much more fun. This sexy, tough warrior version of his mate was one of the best yet. Vohne purred. His heart ached with the power of his love for Kres even as he watched Vohne with wary eyes.

The only glitch in this reunion was trying to figure out why it took so long to return this time. Kings couldn't be identified until they bonded with their mates because memories didn't return until they transformed. Vohne now remembered he always returned as the same human, even as his cat form differed each time. His body was identical because he always matched up with the same bonded. His soul mate. Kres might appear different in each of his reincarnations, but his soul always longed for the same Thresl at his side.

Something must have stopped Vohne's previous reincarnation or there wouldn't be such a gap between his last life and this one. Even as his memories returned, he could feel a big hole in his mind that told him a few incarnations passed where he hadn't found his mate and had never shifted from his Thresl form. Once they reached Nillre, he'd have to investigate and see what had prevented his transformation. Nothing could stand between him and the safety of his mate. Anyone or anything that did would be eliminated.

Looking down at the man he'd loved through millenniums, Vohne pushed all the negativity away. By the time they headed for the castle, every Thresl ever born would know the king and his mate were back, and their enemies had better look out.

Kres put up a token resistance but gave it up as soon as Vohne nipped at his neck. It wasn't the submission of a proper beta. His soldier didn't have enough give in him for that. It was the acknowledgement of letting Vohne have his way because he'd *chosen* to give the Thresl the dominating role.

Vohne didn't know how his mate could get any sexier, but the younger man lying beneath him made his heart swell just as much as he made his cock harden. He barely held back the words of love trying to escape. Kres was already nervous about their bond. Now wasn't the time to tell him this wasn't the first time they'd done this dance.

Vohne leant down and lapped at his lover's neck, scraping his teeth lightly against Kres' skin. Kres shivered, making Vohne smile.

"You are so responsive," Vohne whispered against his throat.

"You are so dead if you don't get on with it," Kres growled.

"I am. I am. Don't get your undies in a bunch." Vohne purred. "Oh wait, you aren't wearing any."

He let his hands roam across the newly exposed skin as he relished the feel of flesh against flesh. *Touch starved*. The phrase danced across his mind. *No…Kres starved*. Not just anyone could soothe Vohne's need for contact. Not just anyone could calm his restless soul—only this man. One special man in a sea of billions of souls.

"I missed you." Vohne flinched as soon as the words were out of his mouth.

Kres gave him an amused smile. "We were only apart for a few hours."

"What can I say? I'm needy." Vohne stopped further comments with a kiss. Nothing was going to stop him from claiming his mate, and he knew Kres would have tons of questions if the truth were known. Vohne would confess everything *after* they completed the bond. Right now wasn't the time to get into a metaphysical discussion.

At the touch of Kres' mouth, Vohne's body came alive. Moaning, he rubbed against his mate's pebbled abs, searching for the perfect friction to end the uncontrollable yearning he felt for him.

Calloused hands gripped his hips, stilling his motion. A snarl burst from his lips.

"Stop it," Kres commanded, his brown eyes firm.

"I need you." Vohne's voice was gravelly with desire, the words almost indistinguishable.

"I know." Kres kissed Vohne's cheek. The first spontaneous show of affection from his mate sent tremors through Vohne's body.

"I need to be inside you," he confessed.

"You need to get undressed first." Kres' lips formed a soft smile that Vohne had to concentrate hard to resist. If he focused on his mate's mouth, he'd never get undressed.

Vohne stripped off his clothing without regard to reusability. The sound of fabric tearing didn't distract him from watching his mate retrieve a tube of lubricant from a box under the bed. "Planning, were you?"

"I did a little shopping while you were out. I knew you would want to claim me when you returned. You aren't exactly shy about saying what you need." Kres' wry grin made Vohne growl. Everything about his soldier excited Vohne.

"I'll never be shy about desiring you." It was best that Kres knew the truth. Vohne would always crave him, and he wouldn't be denied. Well, Kres could, but he hoped his mate wouldn't turn him away without reason. The Thresl-human mating was too intense for some matches. Luckily this was one mating that never had those kinds of problems. They'd had lots of other issues throughout the years, but sexual compatibility had never been one of them.

Vohne's attention snapped to his mate when Kres tried to wriggle away.

Vohne growled.

"You have to give me enough space to use the lube." Kres' brow wrinkled in a frustrated frown.

"No. That's my privilege." He gave his mate a look that he hoped conveyed his confusion over Kres' actions. "You really do need to read that book about Thresls."

"I keep trying to," Kres snapped.

"Thresls take their responsibilities seriously. From now on everything about you is mine to care for. Your body, your happiness — they are all mine."

"Yeah," Kres panted. "And what is my responsibility?"

"To not get killed." A responsibility his lover hadn't always taken seriously, with disastrous consequences. But not this time. This time Vohne was going to keep him safe.

Kres froze beneath Vohne's hands. "What?"

"Never mind." Now wasn't the time to go over years of heartache and humour. Now was the time to solidify their relationship and renew their commitment to each other. Kissing his mate, Vohne made a silent pledge. The same vow he'd made innumerable times before.

Forever. This time I will keep him forever.

Running his mouth down his lover's hard stomach, Vohne licked every sexy ridge. He enjoyed this tougher version of his mate. Joy bubbled through Vohne's veins like Nillrenian wine. They would win this time…

A sharp pain brought his head up.

"Ouch."

Kres gave a short laugh. "What are you thinking about?"

"Your hot body."

"I don't think so. It's like a humming in my mind," Kres explained.

"Talk later. Hot loving now." To keep Kres distracted, he swallowed his lover's cock, taking Kres' entire length to the back of his throat. There was plenty of time to discuss their past. Concentrating on their future was more important.

Kres gave a strangled scream.

Vohne purred. Clamping his hands around Kres' hips, he kept his mate still while he enjoyed the flavour of the man who tasted like the best of everything and owned Vohne's heart.

"I'm going to come," Kres warned.

"Excellent."

He sent the word to his mate, letting him know it was all right. Tasting his lover's essence was his goal. His right. Only his. The strong body beneath him jolted, giving up its delicious fluid. Gripping Kres' hips, Vohne held him still while he sucked at the liquid. When he finally let Kres' cock leave his mouth, Vohne lapped with his rough tongue like a cat at the sticky drips he'd missed.

Kres panted, sucking in gasping breaths to fill his lungs. "I wanted to last longer."

His mate's eyes glowed like small suns, a sign of their bonding. As they grew closer, their powers would multiply. The stronger they bonded, the more powerful they'd become. This time there was no hesitation in Vohne's mind. Lessons from the past had been well learnt, at great consequence. Conquer their enemies or perish—there was no in-between. With his feral blood burning in his veins, Vohne smiled at his lover.

"Don't worry, mate. We just got started," he promised.

Chapter Six

The planet of Nillre shone like a jewel in space. Flashes of blue and gold greeted the spacecraft slowly drifting towards its surface.

"It's beautiful, isn't it?" Vohne's warm breath drifted across Kres' bare flesh, making him shiver. Bumps tingled across his skin at the other man's proximity. Sliding his fingers across the cheek so close to his own, he felt Vohne's beard stubble growing out.

At his touch, Vohne purred, rubbing his face against Kres' hand. "You can stroke me anytime, lover."

Kres laughed. "That is possibly the worst line, ever."

Vohne laughed, warm puffs of air across Kres' ear.

Kres turned his head a fraction, enough for their lips to brush across each other. Sparks of need danced up and down his spine, tightening his body.

The pilot's voice came over the speakers. "We are now approaching the planet of Nillre. Please strap in."

Kres groaned his disappointment, but obediently settled back into his seat. Vohne growled and paced the aisle.

"What are you doing? You heard the pilot."

Vohne glanced out of the window, around the cabin, and out of the window again, but he didn't sit down.

"Vohne, strap in."

There were no other passengers besides the two of them. It was a private shuttle provided by the planet of Nillre to welcome back their king. Only ten luxurious landing chairs filled the entire shuttle where fifty might crowd together in a military craft. After Vohne had contacted them, they couldn't do enough. Unfortunately, Vohne had been unable to reach his brother, who'd been out when he'd called. Kres knew the lack of communication from Vohne's brother bothered his Thresl.

Kres made sure all his buckles and snaps were fastened as he kept a wary eye on his lover. "What's the matter?" Vohne's pacing spiked his nerves.

"Something is wrong," Vohne growled.

"What do you mean?"

Vohne pinned Kres with his amber gaze. "Don't you feel it?"

"All I feel is the ship descending. You need to get strapped in," Kres insisted. He didn't want to see his lover bouncing around the shuttle and possibly injured.

The man-cat's eyes widened. "We need to get you out of here."

"What?"

Kres didn't have time to argue or ask what the hell was going on. Vohne's claws came out. In two swipes, he shredded Kres' harness.

"Stop that." Kres frowned at Vohne's behaviour.

"No. You have to leave." The playful man of seconds ago vanished behind the cold amber gaze.

"I am leaving—as soon as we land," Kres replied, trying to keep his voice calm and level. He'd learnt the calmer he was, the better Vohne responded. If Kres became hysterical it would be all over.

Vohne shook his head. "This shuttle will never land."

"What?"

Kres struggled as Vohne grabbed his arm, dragging him down the centre aisle.

"Stop it. What the fuck is going on? Stop," Kres demanded.

His words fell on deaf ears as Vohne continued dragging Kres to the back of the ship. With his free hand, Vohne typed in a complicated code. A concealed door sprang open.

Vohne grabbed Kres' chin, forcing him to meet his eyes. "You must survive. No matter what, don't trust anyone. I will find you."

"No," Kres protested. He didn't like where this was going. The look in Vohne's eyes freaked him out.

"Yes." Hard lips met his in a brutal, marking kiss. "You have been mine for centuries, and you will be mine again. Don't lose faith."

Running the words through his head, Kres was unprepared for the hard shove that propelled him into the escape pod. A whoosh of sound followed as the door closed behind him.

"Vohne!" Kres pounded on the door, screaming. "Vohne!"

The captain's voice came over the intercom. "Your Highness, my radar has picked up two incoming ships. They must be your welcoming fleet."

"Somehow I doubt it," Vohne responded. "Fire the pod."

Kres scrambled to find the intercom. Pressing the button, he shouted into the receiver. "Don't you dare!"

Vohne's order overrode his. "Fire it, Captain, or I will have you court-martialled."

Fuck!

"Sorry, sir," the captain said. "I have to follow orders."

Kres understood the captain's dilemma, but he didn't have to like it. "If anything happens to Vohne, I will be coming for you."

There was a long pause before the captain spoke again, "Understood, sir."

A loud bang shook the pod. Kres thought at first it was the pod disengaging, until the captain's voice came over the intercom.

"We're being fired upon," the captain said in a calm voice. "What would you like me to do, Your Highness?"

"Eject the pod, Captain," Vohne ordered.

"Vohne!" Kres pounded on the door. He was going to kill the bastard when he got out of there.

"Pod ejecting," a robotic voice announced.

"Travel well, my love." Vohne's words were followed by another explosion, then the pod broke free—but was he free because the captain had ejected the escape pod or because the ship was destroyed?

"Vohne," Kres whispered, sinking to the floor of the shuttle. Now what was he going to do?

* * * *

Vohne let out a relieved sigh as he heard the pod disengage. Closing his eyes, he prayed to the gods to deliver his beloved to the planet below. If Kres didn't survive, neither would he.

"Please let Kres make it safely," he whispered to whatever deity might be listening. He'd have to ask Kres about his beliefs later.

Another explosion rocked the shuttle.

"They're putting a tracking beam on the shuttle, Your Highness," the captain announced.

"Let them." Vohne hoped it kept them distracted. He needed Kres to make it to the surface. He didn't think he could survive this reincarnation if he lost his lover so early.

The shaking of the small craft told Vohne the shuttle was truly caught. He leaned against the smooth ship walls and breathed slow breaths to calm his inner beast. Whiffs of his lover still filled the cabin, soothing his nerves. He had to believe Kres would make it to safety and forgive him for putting him in the escape pod.

He had no illusions about his lover giving him a piece of his mind once they were reunited down below, but as long as they were together again, he didn't care what punishment Kres wanted to dish out.

A loud clang shook him out of his imagined reunion. Squaring his shoulders, he braced himself to face whatever came through the door.

The captain's voice came over the intercom. "Should I let them in?"

"Might as well. If they break in, they'll only damage the shuttle," Vohne replied. No point in fighting with ships when they were outmanned.

A whoosh heralded the opening of the inner door.

Ten soldiers marched through. Seeing Vohne, they stopped in their tracks, staring at him as if they'd seen a ghost.

Vohne drew himself up to full height. "Is there a reason you're attacking your king?"

One of the Thresls, braver than the others, stepped forward, sweeping a low bow. "Forgive us, Your Highness. We were told an imposter was on board." The man's voice shook as he confronted his king.

Vohne's eyes scanned the group who'd entered the shuttle, five male human soldiers and six Thresl. The one who approached didn't appear to have a partner.

"Where's your human?" He asked the brave soldier.

"He died in The Great Purge. As I am only half Thresl, I survived."

"Ahh. I am sorry." At his transformation, Vohne regained all of his memories and the memories of his people. As a king, he was one of the few Thresl who could retain the history of his people. Which made this last return unusual because he had gaps in his memory, spots where he couldn't detect bits and pieces of his past.

While between reincarnations, a faction had arisen that wanted to free the Thresl from their human counterparts. One Thresl mating gone wrong had created a bitter and dangerous man who'd wanted to put an end to what he considered the oppression of the Thresl. What the leader didn't acknowledge was, without humans, there were no Thresl. The original Thresl had bonded with a human in order to become a reasoning, intelligent being and not a slave to his beast. To break from the humans and other sentient creatures was to bring an end to their own sentience.

The Great Purge had been the product of this twisted leader who killed the Thresls' partners. His thinking had been, once a Thresl gained its sentient status, a human partner was no longer necessary.

After killing many Thresl mates, the leader and his followers had learnt a powerful and painful lesson. Without their creators, they were only half a person.

Many killed themselves, and the ones who didn't went insane.

"How did you survive?" Even a half-Thresl would have problems.

The soldier shivered. "I had conditioning. I'm hoping to rematch."

In some cases, if they were rematched quickly, a soldier could stay in his human form for a few months. If they didn't find a Thresl for him soon, he would go into a cryogenic chamber until they found a match. Last Vohne remembered, there were still dozens of Thresls frozen on the planet.

"Good luck," Vohne said even as he shivered over the fate of the man before him.

"Thank you, Your Highness. I have orders to bring the imposter to the ship. Would you mind accompanying me?"

As politely as the soldier had worded the question, Vohne still knew he wouldn't leave without him.

"Of course," Vohne complied. He didn't want to make it difficult for the men. They weren't the ones in charge of the orders to shoot Vohne from the sky. However, if anything hurt Kres, or if he died before he made it to the planet, all bets were off.

The soldiers formed an honour guard around Vohne, now acting as his protection instead of his captors.

"Don't forget to bring the captain aboard," Vohne reminded. He didn't know if the shuttle was still space-worthy and he didn't want the captain to be forgotten in their rush to take Vohne aboard the larger vessel.

"Of course, Your Highness," another guard replied.

Vohne yearned to immediately seek out Kres, but he still didn't know if it was safe.

Through several winding hallways he marched alongside the soldiers until finally he was brought to a large, luxurious chamber covered in thick carpet, with a strong handsome man sitting behind a desk.

Looking straight into those familiar gold eyes, Vohne gave a wide smile. "Greetings, brother."

Bleine, Vohne's younger brother, stood up, walked over to Vohne, then with brutal strength, punched him in the face.

Vohne's head snapped back, his hand coming up to cup his injured cheek. "What the hell did you do that for?"

"For waiting so fucking long to come back! I had to go through an entire war without you. Where the hell have you been?"

Vohne looked into his brother's eyes and knew the past hundred years had been hard on him. Without tragedy, a Thresl could live for centuries, even though only kings went through reincarnation.

"I don't know! Why did you shoot at me?"

"Because Jallryne said a false king would be coming."

"Who's Jallryne?" Vohne asked. The name didn't sound familiar.

"My human. She's a seer." His brother paled at the realisation — he had been manipulated.

"What happened to Klia?" Vohne had liked his brother's last partner. She'd been a tiny caramel-haired woman with an easy laugh.

"She died in the purging. Jallryne was my second attempt. We bonded, but now I'm wondering if I chose incorrectly." A frown marred Bleine's smooth face.

"You think she likes being queen too much?" Vohne asked. Jallryne wouldn't be the first person to go mad with power.

"Maybe. There have been whispered rumours, but I thought it was just court jealousy. The castle is a different place without you, brother. I never took the official title of king. It didn't feel right since I wasn't a true one." Bleine gripped Vohne's shoulder, shaking him slightly. "I always knew you would return, even as others doubted."

Fear churned Vohne's stomach. He didn't want there to be a civil war over his return. "How will my reception be?"

"It had better be welcoming." Bleine's cold tone indicated nothing less would be acceptable to him. "However, it is a tumultuous time. A struggle for power is underway. There are others who would love to wrest the throne from me and call themselves king. Your long absence has brought out many contenders who would never dare to challenge the throne if you were there."

"We'll put them back in their place and discover who's been working against us," Vohne declared.

In his heart, he knew his brother was beside him.

"Where's your mate?" Bleine looked behind him.

"You tried to blow up my shuttle. Where do you think he is?" Vohne growled. He still hadn't forgiven his brother for that.

"Y-you sent him down below without protection?" Bleine's panicked expression sent a shard of fear through Vohne.

"Since when does a mate need protection from my people?" he asked.

"Since there are those who would love to capture him and use him against the newly awakened king," Bleine countered.

"Anyone who touches him will die by my hand," Vohne snarled. The idea of someone hurting Kres made him want to turn feral.

Bleine shook his head. "That still won't bring him back, and sadly, there are many who will die for their cause. Besides, even if they don't kill him, they might hold him for ransom or just hold him over your head."

Vohne let out a short laugh as he remembered how his mate had handled the last battle. There had been no shortage of people willing to tell Vohne of Kres' ruthlessness. "Holding my mate will be more trouble than they might expect."

Bleine frowned. "In the past, he's always been a dreamer."

"Not his time." Vohne smiled. "This time he's a warrior."

Bleine's expression was one of utter horror. "Then the prophecy is true."

"What are you talking about?" His brother had always been the bookish one, while Vohne was the fighter.

"All the time you were gone, I searched the vault for reasons you weren't brought back. I couldn't understand why you hadn't resurfaced yet. One of the oldest manuscripts I could find said that even for the king there is a final reincarnation. It will occur when your people need you the most."

"They needed me during The Great Purge," Vohne growled. "I let them down by not returning. Something must've prevented me from coming back."

That was the only thing Vohne could think of. An outside force had stopped him from returning and finding his mate in order to prevent the purge.

Bleine nodded. "Which makes me worry about what's coming now. It said that in the final reincarnation the king's mate will be a warrior. I shared this with Jallryne. If she is the deceiver like we believe, she'll be on the lookout for your mate. If he dies, this time he won't come back."

Fear rushed through Vohne. "We need to make sure that doesn't happen. Get this ship landed. I have to find my mate!"

* * * *

It took several deep breaths and many images about the revenge he was going to take on his mate before Kres pulled it together. Picking himself up off the floor, he assessed the pod. With no idea of what situation he might land in, he popped open the provision chamber and scanned the contents.

"Great!"

Finally, something was going his way. The chamber was fully stocked.

The usual amenities lay inside. Food, jugs of water, snack bars, and tucked in the back, a military style survival dagger. Kres snatched up the dagger, tucked it in his boot, and filled his pockets with bars before cracking open a bottle of water. He needed to stay hydrated in case there wasn't a lot of water where he landed. Damn, he wished he'd asked Vohne more about his home planet instead of concentrating on getting into his pants.

He paced the pod, occasionally glancing at the monitor to judge when he would land. If Vohne survived, he would go to the palace. Kres couldn't even think of the possibility of his lover's death. If Vohne were dead, he'd know.

A computerised voice came over the intercom. "Impact in five minutes."

Kres sat back down and fastened the seat buckle tight.

"You're keeping secrets from me, man-cat," Kres mused. Thinking over the hints and bits the Thresl had dropped, he worried about what the shifter hadn't shared.

"Impact in three minutes."

Sighing, Kres leaned his head back and closed his eyes. What the hell had happened to his life? A few days ago, he'd been more than happy to be a common soldier. Now he was a Thresl-mate to a king—a king who may or may not be alive.

"You have to be alive," he whispered. Luckily he didn't get much time to fixate on his lover's plight— not while hurtling towards a planet in a small capsule.

"Impact in one minute."

The pod slammed into the ground, bounced, and slammed into the ground again before rolling. When the pod finally stopped, Kres' insides were churning and his jaws ached from clenching his teeth.

He let out a breath of relief when the pod landed right side up.

After a few coping breaths to settle his nerves, Kres unbuckled the safety harness with shaky fingers. He grabbed another bottle of water before he walked to the pod door. Programmed to release its occupants after landing, the door popped open at his approach.

"Sure, now you open," he grumbled, glaring at the silver orb. He wished it had opened back on the ship where he could've grabbed Vohne to go with him. He was going to punch his mate in the face the next time he saw him. Vohne damn well better be safe and sound for Kres' abuse.

Peeking out of the pod, Kres saw nothing but grass, trees and a stone path. A long burn pattern scarred the earth from his landing.

"Looks like I'm walking," he muttered.

He'd only taken a few steps towards the path when the sound of electronic thrumming filled the air. A whoosh of air accompanied the landing of a luxury air ship. It was a private ship, only sixty feet long, emblazoned with a crest on the side.

Vohne.

Kres' heartbeat doubled in speed. Surely this would be the type of ship a king took.

Relief lightened his heart. He waited patiently for the ship to finish landing and the door to open. A pang of disappointment stabbed through his chest when a woman descended from the transportation, followed by a cadre of official looking guards.

The woman approached him with a wide smile. "I was told you were on your way, King-Mate. I'm Jallryne. Welcome home."

Kres watched her approach, saw her enchanting smile and knew.

This is the enemy.

It was the expression in her eyes. As a soldier he'd learnt to identify hidden motives and unfriendly opponents. She almost vibrated with rage. The closer she came with the armed men at her back the tighter his nerves became. He resisted the urge to go for his knife. Instead, he stayed as still as he could, calling upon hidden resources of control.

"I heard from my mate. The king is well and on his way to the castle. I'm to bring you to him."

Hearing that news from anyone else, Kres would have jumped up and down with joy, but he didn't want to get into that ship with her. He knew with a soldier's instinct, if he boarded that ship, he wouldn't come out.

His gaze slid over her shoulder at the men standing at attention behind her.

The soldier on her left looked him in the eyes. "*Run*," the man mouthed.

Kres' nerves snapped. Turning on his heel, he fled.

A scream of rage followed his disappearance. He headed towards the trees. He needed cover and needed it right then. A few stray blasts landed too close, scarring the ground beside him. From their proximity he knew it was from the soldier who had told him to flee.

Anyone who could shoot could have easily hit him at such close range. Not all the soldiers were on her side. Unfortunately, it only took one good shot to kill a man who had nothing but a knife to defend himself.

Long forgotten survivalist training rushed back into his mind as his feet found the quiet earth. He instinctively missed the crunchy leaves and rustling undergrowth as he ran. If the deceitful bitch wasn't lying, Vohne lived.

If Vohne lived, he would find Kres. Kres just had to survive long enough for the reunion.

"You shouldn't be alive. She promised me you couldn't return!" the woman screamed behind him.

A thick tree with low branches caught his eye. With a desperate leap, Kres grabbed the lowest branch, tucking his body close to the trunk. With slow, careful movements, he pulled himself to the branch above, his muscles screaming from the strain. Long, draping vines covered the space between branches, protecting him from spying eyes.

Kres was reluctant to attack any of the soldiers. He didn't know which ones shared the warning soldier's views and which ones wanted to see his blood sprayed across the ground.

The woman was easy.

She wanted him dead.

If she came close enough, he would slit her throat with no remorse.

From his informal count of men rustling through the underbrush, there were ten of them along with the woman. He longed for his stun gun with a passion.

"Come out, King-Mate. Once you're gone, there will be no more problems. Once you're gone, there will be no more king. He'll never be able to survive your death this time."

Shit, she was going to hurt Vohne. Kres hoped if he didn't survive this, Vohne would be all right. The man-cat had said they needed more time together to be completely bonded. Kres hoped that would increase Vohne's chances of living if the psycho bitch killed Kres.

Kres' mind went completely blank as his nerves vanished and a warrior's calm took over.

She'd threatened his mate.

She must die.

Kres crouched among the leaves. Spreading his feet, he centred himself and steadied his balance, ready to spring and take her down. The soldiers might shoot him after, but he'd take out the danger to his mate first.

He silently slid the knife out of his boot, careful to keep his movements slow and quiet. Peering through the foliage, he watched her approach.

"Come out, King-Mate. As soon as my people at the castle take care of your mate, the pair of you can reunite in the afterlife. Maybe then he can keep better track of you."

Kres blocked out her words. He wasn't going to let her trick him into revealing his location. A bug buzzed past his ear. Kres didn't move, nor did he twitch when something bit him on the neck.

A few more steps.

She was directly beneath the trunk of the tree where he hid. Taking a slow breath, he bunched his muscles, ready to leap. A series of blasts sounded through the forest. The woman's body flung back, ricocheted off the tree, then lay still.

One of the soldiers peered over at the woman. "Who shot her?"

"I did." A blond soldier walked up, approaching the body.

"I don't think so." A dark-haired soldier marched over. "See that mark through her heart. That's mine." He sounded ridiculously proud.

"Not so," the blond argued. "See that shot in her forehead. That killed her. I win."

"Hmm." The man who'd told Kres to run looked down at the body. The others deferred to him as the leader. "We'll have to have the coroner examine the body. That will determine the winner."

Kres stilled. *They're having a contest about who killed her?*

"What about the king-mate?" one of the soldiers asked.

"We have to find him. If we return without him, we'd best plan on living in the prison yards," the leader said.

The blond spoke up. "What if he isn't worthy? We should have a plan. I've never even met the king."

Kres had heard enough. Dangling from his perch, he dropped down behind the blond. Wrapping his right arm around the soldier's neck, he used his left hand to hold the knife blade close to the man's eyes.

"Don't even think about harming my mate," he warned. With a backwards snap of his foot, he knocked out the soldier trying to sneak up on him. The man fell to the ground with a thump. "I wouldn't do that," he warned as he locked eyes with the leader, who stared back with a cautious expression.

"No need to kill him, King-Mate. He's just talking like soldiers do. He wasn't going to harm the king. Were you, Friln?"

Kres lifted the knife a fraction to let the blond speak.

"No, sir, I wouldn't harm your mate."

Kres heard the truth in the other man's voice. "I'm not inclined to like you people very much," he said in a hard tone.

"I thought you said he was a gentle soul," another soldier said to the leader. "He doesn't look so gentle to me."

"I'm Nelrin, the captain of the guard. The man you have under your knife is my mate Friln. I'd prefer if you didn't kill him."

"Did you really get a message that the king is alive?" Kres asked.

Nelrin gave him a surprised look. "Yes. I heard it myself." His voice turned coaxing. "Come with us and we'll take you to him."

"Give me one of your weapons."

The leader held out his weapon towards Kres, handle first. Kres released Friln, shoving him towards

Nelrin. He snatched the weapon when the leader grabbed at his mate.

Kres dropped the knife back into his boot and flipped the weapon to point at the soldiers. He carefully examined each of them before he lowered the blaster.

"If any of you plan on hurting my mate, think again. Now get me to the king."

Without another glance at the soldiers, Kres turned around and headed back to the shuttle.

He'd almost reached the shuttle when the world started to spin. His skin burned, itched, burned again.

With a gasp he dropped the gun.

As the light started to dim, he heard one of the soldiers curse. "Shit, he's been bit. He's going into shock. We've got to get him back to the palace."

Everything went black.

* * * *

"I heard from the palace. Your mate is having an allergic reaction to a Syphin sting."

Vohne shook his head. "Poor thing. Did they give him an inoculation?"

"Yeah, he's fine now, but apparently he's ready to hand you your balls on a platter," Bleine said with a grin.

"I'm not surprised." Vohne smiled. "He's tough." He wasn't worried. Syphin bites were brutal, but they'd long ago created a shot that easily reversed the symptoms.

"Not so tough a little bug can't take him down," Bleine taunted.

Sweat beaded his brother's forehead. Ignoring Bleine's teasing, Vohne looked more carefully at his sibling. "Are you feeling all right? You look pale."

"No. My soldiers did their job. I offered them a reward if they disposed of Jallryne. When we land, find out who killed her. The killer is your new captain of the guard. I had to make sure your right-hand man was loyal, and Jallryne had to die to discover where their loyalties lie."

A sick churning spun Vohne's stomach. Rushing over, he grabbed his brother's arm and lowered him back to his chair. "You can survive this. She was a bad match," he urged.

"No. My time is over. I only lived to see you return to your throne. It isn't my fate to live any longer. I outlived my first mate and now my second. It's time for me to fade into the stars."

"I can't let you leave me, brother," Vohne growled.

Bleine gave a thready laugh. "Some things even you can't control, brother. Watch your back. Jallryne had accomplices."

Vohne ran to the intercom. "Medic!" he shouted into the speaker. "I need a medic with a cryogenic processor."

"Immediately, Your Highness," a tinny voice responded.

"What are you doing?" Bleine asked. His brother's skin turned an unnatural greyish tint before Vohne's eyes.

"I'm going to freeze you until I can find you a new mate."

Bleine laughed, a bare whisper of a sound. "You're insane."

"Maybe, but I can't lose you. Not now. You're all the family I have left." He couldn't lose his brother right after they'd been reunited. He just couldn't.

"You have your mate," Bleine reminded him, his voice barely above a whisper.

Vohne nodded. "I know but he's not blood. I can't lose you, Bleine. All the others are long gone. We are the last of our line."

"You have to have children. I left you a list at the castle."

"A list of what?"

"Of appropriate king bearers. Choose one and get her pregnant. There are several half-Thresls who would do nicely," Bleine said.

Vohne laughed, even as he felt tears forming in his eyes. "If I got some girl pregnant, I wouldn't have to worry about being the last of my line. My mate would fillet me."

"I didn't say touch the girl. There are many other ways. Besides, you will want a child or your mate's also," Bleine commented as if he thought it weird Vohne hadn't thought of that himself.

Vohne imagined a little girl with Kres' beautiful eyes and felt his heart melt. Bleine coughed, a deep hacking sound as if he were spitting out his soul. Vohne rushed to his brother's side and helped him to the floor, just as the doors swung open and a medical team marched inside.

"I want him frozen. We'll keep him in storage until we can find him a replacement," he commanded.

"Vohne, don't do this. Let me go," Bleine insisted. "It's my time."

"No!" He turned his attention to the medic. "Do what I said."

"But, Your Highness, if he doesn't want to be frozen..." the man unwisely protested.

"I am the king. Do as I say." He turned back to his brother. "Bleine, don't fight me on this. I will seek you out a new mate with the help of the advisors. Surely we can find one person to be yours."

Bleine stared at him for so long Vohne thought he would have to fight his dying brother. Finally, Bleine nodded.

"Do it," he commanded the medics who quickly rushed to comply.

Vohne stood up, stepping aside as the medical team placed his brother in the metal cylinder. A small clear window allowed him to watch the freezing gas fill the chamber. Bleine's gaze linked with his until his brother blinked no more, his frozen eyes focusing on nothing.

"Goodbye, brother," Vohne whispered. A sense of incredible loss filled him. He hadn't even made it back to his kingdom and already he had a long to-do list. Oust the people who plotted against him, reunite with his mate, find his brother a mate of his own, and try to avoid Kres' knife when he discovered Vohne was looking for a surrogate to bear his children.

It was going to be a busy, busy time.

Chapter Seven

Vohne all but raced off the shuttle, his eyes scanning the landing area for his mate.

Ignoring the line of people eager to get a look at their king, Vohne moved through the crowd searching for Kres.

"I'm right here."

Vohne turned around. Pain exploded across his nose. "Ow, you hit me." He shook his head to get rid of the ringing in his ears.

"You shoved me into that damned pod, knowing you could die. Don't you ever do that to me again!" Kres' eyes glowed with rage.

Vohne blocked out the pain. Gripping his mate's handsome face between his hands, he forced Kres to meet his eyes. "I love you too."

Not giving Kres a chance to reply, he crushed his mate's mouth with his lips. Kres' unique flavour exploded across his tongue. Licking inside, he wallowed in the taste and scent of his man.

Mine.

To have his strong mate in his arms again soothed Vohne's inner beast. Kres' heart thrummed beneath his touch. "I'm sorry I sent you away, but I'd do it again if your life was threatened."

His mate's eyes narrowed. "I should've hit you harder."

Vohne laughed. Wrapping his arms tight around his mate, he breathed in the scent of the one person in the universe who represented everything perfect in his life. Kres smelt like home.

"Your Highness?" Vohne looked up to see a large Thresl soldier standing behind Kres.

"Yes?"

"Your mate is still weak from the bite. He needs to rest," the soldier scolded with a frown at Kres.

Vohne leant back to get a good look at Kres. His mate lifted an eyebrow at him. "I'm well enough to kick your butt."

He kissed the tip of his mate's nose. "I love it when you get feisty."

"You might like it less with my boot up your ass."

Vohne's sharp hearing picked up the quickly stifled laughter of the soldier standing at attention behind Kres' right shoulder.

"What's your name, soldier?"

"I am Nelrin, captain of the guard, or at least until you assign someone else," the soldier replied.

"My brother said the man who killed his mate would be my captain," Vohne stated.

Nelrin nodded. "We are still investigating who killed her. Until then I will be happy to stand in place of your future captain. My mate is one of the contenders for the title." He waved a beckoning hand towards the crowd, and a blond human joined the other man. Vohne could tell they were a matched pair.

"We will meet and discuss strategy in the morning. First I need to reconnect with my man," Vohne growled. No one would get in the way of his bonding with Kres. At that moment, he needed his mate more than oxygen.

"I'd be honoured to show you to your rooms," Nelrin courteously replied.

"I'd be happy for the escort." He had difficulty concentrating on anyone other than Kres when they were together. Vohne took his mate's arm, leading his mercurial lover along with him.

"I'm still mad at you," Kres whispered.

"Good, we can have make-up sex." Nothing would deter him. He had both his home and his mate in the same location—Kres would be lucky if they made it back to their room and Vohne didn't take his lover on the floor in front of the entire palace.

Kres laughed. Vohne knew he needed to clear things up with his lover and find out what had happened after his mate had landed, but his body yearned for the man of his heart and he wouldn't be denied.

He nodded politely to anyone he passed, dragging Kres along after him.

"Here you go, Your Highness." Nelrin and his mate both bowed as the pair passed into the room.

Vohne slammed the door in the soldiers' faces, ignoring the snickers from the other side. Juveniles.

Turning to his mate, he let out a growl. "Why are you still dressed?"

Kres rolled his eyes. "Because we've been here about five seconds, and I didn't think you wanted me to strip in front of your soldiers."

Vohne snarled at his mate. "They are our soldiers, and I don't care what they see as long as they don't touch." He marched over to his mate and ripped Kres' shirt in half. "You are mine, and I'll challenge anyone who tries to take you from me." Possessive before, now his feral nature pushed at him to claim his man. "There is one thing you should learn about Thresls, my love. Humans might form us, but make no mistake, you belong to my beast."

* * * *

Kres melted beneath his mate's hands and mouth. All the angry words saved for this moment vanished as his mind went blank and his body pliant. Moans rolled up his throat in a fair imitation of a Thresl purr.

"Yours. Anything." His bones damned near melted beneath his lover's onslaught. "Mmmm." Eyes rolling to the back of his head, Kres' body tried to mould to his mate.

A loud tearing sound and a sudden breeze alerted him to the absence of his pants. Pulling away, he glanced down. "How come I'm naked but you're still dressed?"

Vohne gave him a toothy smile. "I'm just lucky I guess."

Flexing his powerful muscles, the Thresl picked Kres up and carried him to the bed where he laid Kres down with tender care. Vohne looked at him with such love in his eyes that Kres blinked back tears.

"Don't cry, my love. I will never leave you, never lose you, and never care for another as long as I live. Our souls were entwined at the dawn of time, and we will be together until it ends," Vohne vowed.

Kres gave his lover a watery smile. "Strip, gorgeous. I need to bond."

Vohne purred. "Anything for you, my mate."

First he peeled off his shirt, exposing his smooth skin and rippled abs, then with a sexy swagger, he unfastened his pants, dropping them with little fanfare. The lack of underwear was almost as sexy as the expression of lust and love on his mate's face.

There was no doubt in Kres' mind—Vohne loved him.

When the larger man slid across him, Kres' back bowed with the sensation. Tingles of want and need sparked a firestorm of desire throughout his body. "Fuck me," he whispered over the lump in his throat.

The gentle touch of his mate seared his soul.

A soft rustling had him snapping his eyes open, eyes he hadn't realised had been closed.

Vohne gave him a wide smile. "Just getting something to slick you up, my love."

"Hurry or I'll finish without you." It wouldn't take much effort either. His body was primed.

A low laugh met his words. "Hold on, my darling." Slowly, one finger then two filled Kres, replacing the gaping emptiness he'd felt over their separation.

"More." Not enough. He needed more.

"Patience, lover."

"Don't make me hurt you," Kres snarled at the teasing glint in his lover's eyes.

"You wouldn't hurt me, because then I couldn't do this." Vohne pressed the tip of his cock at the entrance of Kres' hole.

"Please," Kres begged, pushing into the sensation. "I need you."

"You have me, always." Vohne filled his lover slowly as Kres gasped and writhed on his lover's cock.

"More."

"Shhh. I want to savour this moment."

"Savour it any more and I'll introduce you to my new knife," Kres snapped.

Vohne laughed as he entered Kres, causing an odd sensation, but Kres didn't care. Finally, the Thresl filled him.

"Fuck me!" Kres demanded.

"Oh, I will." Vohne gave a throaty purr. With the same excruciating slowness, he moved in and out of his lover until Kres locked his heels behind Vohne's back and impaled himself on his mate's cock.

"Yes," he hissed.

Vohne gave a convulsive pump of his hips. "Sneaky bastard," he growled.

"That's me." He'd given up everything to be with this man. He deserved a reward. "Fuck me like you mean it."

Vohne gave Kres a long, slow kiss. "I always mean it."

With Kres urging him on, Vohne's movements became harder, rougher, until the lovers lost control and the smell of spunk filled the air.

Kres felt a momentary sense of abandonment when Vohne pulled out of his body. A soft cry of protest left him.

"Shhh, love, I'll be right back."

Vohne went through a doorway and returned quickly with a warm cloth. With tender care, he wiped Kres down, letting his love show through his touch. After disposing of the towel, he returned, sliding onto the bed next to Kres.

Vohne's eyes were warm and melty as they looked down at him. Kres smiled.

"I would cross the galaxies to see that smile," Vohne vowed to his mate.

Kres couldn't stop the soft laugh. "You already did."

* * * *

The next morning Kres sneaked out of bed, dressed quickly, and slipped his knife into his right boot. Vohne made a soft sound as he left their bed but otherwise didn't awaken. Kres blew him a kiss before leaving their bedroom. Yesterday he hadn't got much of a chance to look over the castle before his mate had arrived. From what Vohne had said, there were enemies within its walls, and Kres was more than willing to flush them out.

Closing the door, he was startled out of his thoughts by a voice behind him.

"Going somewhere, King-Mate?"

Kres spun around. Nelrin and Friln stood behind him, arms crossed in front of their chests as if they were ready to scold a recalcitrant child.

"Gentlemen." Kres gave the soldiers a respectful nod. "What are you two doing here?"

"The coroner declared Friln the winner. He's your new Captain of the Guard, but as I am the most senior, I came to watch his back. We never travel in less than pairs, preferably with our mate."

"Makes sense." Unfortunately to Kres, it meant two men to distrust at a time instead of one. "Well, go ahead and continue your guard. The king is still asleep inside."

Kres spun on his heel.

Nelrin stepped in his path.

"Is there a problem?" He didn't want to hurt Friln, but he wouldn't be stopped either.

"I doubt the king would approve of you wandering around the castle alone. Let me call a guard for your escort."

Kres gave Nelrin a vicious smile. "The king knows I'm a big boy and can handle walking down the corridor without incident."

"But it could cause a problem," Nelrin argued. "As King-Mate you are the second most valuable person on the planet. There should be a pair of guards with you at all times."

"Well, you'd best get back to guarding the first most valuable person and leave me alone."

Kres shoved Nelrin aside, only to be stopped by a hard grip around his wrist.

"Good morning, my love," Vohne purred. "Going somewhere?"

He could tell by the look in his mate's eyes he'd heard everything.

Vohne saw the determination in Kres' eyes, and his heart sank to his feet. "You can't just go into the court and hunt down anyone who disagrees with me."

Kres gave him a feral smile worthy of a Thresl. "I can if that disagreement leads to them trying to kill you. Somewhere, someone knows who is behind this entire thing, and we know it wasn't just Jallryne. She said someone in the castle was going to finish you. She sounded extremely confident."

"And you think marching around and threatening people will get you the answer you seek? No one is going to raise their hand and say it was them. Planning a coup takes a great deal of stealth."

Kres' beautiful eyes narrowed. "So what should I do then, hmm? Wait around for someone to stab you in the back? Wait for one of your adoring courtiers to poison your food?"

Vohne sighed. It would be difficult to rein in his love. "We have to be discreet."

Nelrin cleared his throat.

"Yes?"

"Pardon, Your Highness, but I've asked around a bit. Since most people couldn't stand Jallryne, I paid attention to those who were most concerned about her death. The royals who expressed the most worry about her demise and your ascension as king were Duke Hellbur and Lady Nelb."

"What do you know about these two?" Kres asked with a frown of concentration on his face.

"There is still the question of what or who prevented me from reawakening. We should've been together the past hundred years. Something stopped us."

Kres' brow furrowed. "What are you talking about? I'm human. I get the one life and then I'm done."

Vohne gave into the temptation to touch his mate, running his fingers through his lover's hair. "You are my Thresl mate, and we are bound by fate, time, and the gods to meet in every lifetime. In the next few months, your memories will return, and you will know all that you've known before. I'd love to know what you did in those lives where we never met."

Kres stepped away from his touch, making Vohne's heart skip a painful beat.

"Are you saying I am born over and over again?" Kres' narrowed gaze warned Vohne he might want to tiptoe around his lover.

"Yes, but according to my brother, this will be our last incarnation," Vohne offered, wondering if that fact made things better.

"So if we die this time and aren't reincarnated, what happens to us?" Kres asked.

"No one knows. I've always thought eventually we become one with the stars like the other Thresls." Vohne's gaze snapped to the guards. Shit, he probably shouldn't have said that out in the open hallway. His enemies would love to get their hands on that type of information. No matter how many times he reincarnated, there was always some power-hungry idiot who thought they could lead the Thresls better.

"Don't worry, the hallway is secure." Nelrin's gaze swept the area. "Any words between you won't pass from me or my mate."

Friln nodded his agreement. "I won't say anything."

"Nevertheless, let's take this into our room." Vohne pulled Kres along, slamming the door in the guards' faces.

"That wasn't polite," Kres commented.

"I don't want them to know everything. The fewer people who know our plans, the better our odds of winning. We don't know who's on our side."

"I still can't believe I reincarnated," Kres said.

"Believe it. However, because we've reincarnated, some of my enemies hold long grudges. I need to reacquaint myself with my old allies and find out who's still loyal. Over the years, people change sides and I won't know until I see them if they're still faithful."

Kres frowned. "So not all Thresls reincarnate?"

Vohne shook his head. "Kings reincarnate—the rest of the Thresls just live extremely long lives. The oldest living Thresl is three thousand years old."

"Wow." He could see Kres trying to wrap his head around that information. He tilted his head curiously. "How will you know by sight?"

"Their scent. Deceit has a certain smell. I have the best nose in the palace, or at least I did. Those who want to destroy me will avoid me so I won't scent their motives. It's important that you stay by my side. I can't lose you, and you won't be able to sort the good people from the bad. Don't go to anyone I haven't approved and keep guards with you at all times." His lover's stubborn expression made his heart sink. "I mean it, Kres. I won't survive if anything happens to you. A Thresl needs his mate, which is why my brother is a frozen princecicle instead of by my side. Others will try to harm you to get to me. Don't give them the opportunity."

Kres gave Vohne a wicked smile. "They will find it harder than they think to kill this human."

Vohne nodded. "Agreed, but I'd prefer you stayed safe by my side."

"Really?" Kres took a step forward, his hungry eyes sweeping Vohne's body. "Because I'd like to stay on top of you, or beneath you, or maybe even inside you. I think I was hasty in leaving our bed this morning."

Vohne swallowed the moisture pooling in his throat as his mate grabbed him, slamming their bodies together. As Kres kissed him with a burning fervour, Vohne's only thought was that he loved this incarnation of his mate, he really did.

* * * *

Two hours later they left their rooms newly showered and dressed. Kres fidgeted beneath the formal clothes his lover had made him wear.

"Stop wiggling," Vohne remonstrated.

"I can't help it." The clothing was restricting. The only saving grace was the high boots that let him bring his knife.

"You need to walk like a king, not wiggle like a little boy." Vohne took one step away from his lover as he finished talking.

"I can still stab you from here," Kres growled.

The Thresl laughed. "Yeah, but you'd miss me too much."

The guards fell into step behind them. "You look real nice, King-Mate," Nelrin said.

"Thank you, Nelrin," Kres said wryly.

"He's right, my mate, you look real pretty." Vohne flashed him a wicked grin.

"I won't miss you when I bury you in the ground," Kres snarled. He hated comments about his looks. He was a soldier, not a model. He gave an extra scowl towards Vohne, who responded with a smile.

Nelrin scooted to stand protectively next to Vohne.

"You can't get me," the king whispered loudly with a wink towards his mate.

"Don't bet on it," Kres grumbled.

The four men walked down the halls until they reached an enormous room with dozens of people milling about. A cheer went up when the crowd caught sight of Vohne.

One man separated from the crowd. His elaborate clothing put Kres' outfit to shame, and his blond hair was brushed to a high sheen. He rushed over to Vohne then knelt before the king.

"My Liege, I'd like to say that I and my house are thrilled at your return. Some said you'd abandoned us, but I knew that day would never come," the blond gushed.

Kres gave Vohne an incredulous look. His mate grinned back. *"Easy, mate,"* Vohne's voice whispered in his head.

Releasing his clenched hands, Kres realised his right hand was creeping towards his knife. When had he turned so violent? Although he'd trained as a soldier, it wasn't until he'd become the Thresl's mate that his more vicious tendencies had come to the forefront.

Anyone who wandered too close to Vohne became the enemy.

"Kreslan, this is Duke Hellbur." He helped the duke up, releasing his hold as soon as the man was on his feet. Walking over to Kres, he put his arm around Kres' waist. "Your Grace, this is my mate, Kreslan Piers."

"Nice to meet you again, King-Mate." The duke gave a low bow.

Kres nodded. "Same here." Vohne's grip tightened on his waist, letting him know his voice was less than sincere.

The duke looked amused at Kres' combative tone. "I'm glad to see you've reunited again. We all worried you wouldn't come back."

"So I hear. Now the question is why it took so long?" Vohne replied.

Hellbur frowned. "What do you mean?"

"Don't you think it a little strange that it took me over a hundred years to return? Not to mention I didn't appear for a major conflict."

The duke straightened his tie as he looked back and forth between Vohne and Kres. "I thought you wanted a break or something. After hundreds of years of rule, you deserved some time off."

"And you thought I'd take it in the middle of a crisis? That I'd let the Thresl mates be purged and not rush home?"

Hellbur paled. "You're right, but in the middle of a war against our mates, it was difficult to think clearly."

"I hear some people want to take his place," Kres grumbled. He didn't like the way the duke looked at his mate.

"There has been some talk." The duke cast an apologetic look at Vohne. "You were gone a long time, Your Highness, but my house is eager to renew our vows to your service."

Vohne gave a nod. "There will be a renewal ceremony tomorrow. It will be interesting to see who shows up."

The duke gave an uncomfortable smile. "There are some who want to go their own way, claiming the monarchy is outdated. Some peoples' memories have faded over time."

This time it was Kres sending calming thoughts to his mate when he felt Vohne start to growl.

"Maybe it's time to remind people why they need a king," Vohne said in a cold voice.

* * * *

Kres spent the rest of the day pretending he was happy to meet people. He wished he had enhanced senses or superpowers or anything to help him sniff out the back-stabbing betrayers. To help catch the court members who'd tried to harm his mate and would try again.

As big as he talked, he could feel Vohne's pain at his people's betrayal. Even though he gave a good front as a calm and confident ruler, Kres could feel the insecurity and hurt Vohne hid just beneath the surface as they walked through the palace greeting people.

Vohne gripped Kres' arm as if reading his unease. Considering their link, maybe Vohne did experience Kres' emotions. He gave his lover a smile.

"Greetings, King and King-Mate." A beautiful woman with shining black hair and sparkling blue eyes curtsied to them. Kres sized her up, wondering if the knife belted around her waist was ornamental or functional. He moved slightly in front of his lover until Vohne tightened his hold and pulled him back.

The woman's mouth quirked into a smile. "I'd heard you were protective, but I hadn't heard the king couldn't take care of himself."

Kres bared his teeth in a facsimile of a smile. "Want me to show you what I can do with your knife?"

She laughed, but he noticed she did add a little space between the king and herself. "I am Niafe, daughter of Lady Nelb. I've come to warn you, Your Highness, my mother means you ill will."

"And you just happened to come by to warn us because you're such a devoted subject?" Kres asked, his voice heavy with sarcasm.

"Easy, mate," Vohne murmured in his ear. "No reason to kill the messenger."

"She's not the messenger. A messenger would be someone carrying a message from one person to another. She's the source," Kres corrected his mate.

"I have a message from my mother," Niafe offered with a shy smile.

Vohne gave Kres a smug look.

Kres scuffed his boot on the ground then afterwards felt guilty. Some worker would probably stay up all night obsessing about that smudge on the surface of his shiny boots. Maybe he'd hide them when he got back to the room.

"Focus, Kres," Vohne admonished. "What's your mother's message, my lady?"

"I'm supposed to stab your mate." She announced the words like she should be given a medal for not following her mother's directive.

Vohne shoved Kres behind him. "And why didn't you?"

Niafe laughed. "Two reasons. First, I've read the old texts and I don't follow her beliefs. And second, your mate's knife looks bigger than mine."

Chapter Eight

They pulled Niafe into an empty room to minimise the number of people who could listen in. The guards blocked the door after a moment of argument. Neither of them trusted Niafe alone with the king and his mate, but Vohne insisted.

Unable to override the orders of their king, the soldiers reluctantly waited outside.

"You're very brave to meet me alone," Niafe said.

Vohne shrugged. "As you stated, my mate has a very large knife. You make the wrong move, and he'll gut you."

Niafe paled, giving Kres a nervous look. Vohne felt a momentary pang of guilt for making it appear as though his mate was seconds from snapping, but the look Kres gave Niafe had him holding back a laugh. His lover was extremely protective.

"Don't worry. As long as you don't make any sudden movements, you're safe enough," Kres assured her.

"Why don't we sit down?" Vohne motioned towards the table and chairs. They'd wandered into one of the meeting rooms the scholars generally used for studies. From the cobwebs decorating the ceiling, he had a feeling it had been a while since anyone had concentrated on learning. Vohne made a mental note to get the scholars back on track. A society that didn't focus on learning would falter. He wondered how much knowledge had been lost in the purge. Shaking his head, he focused on the task at hand. There would be time later to concentrate on the future of Thresl civilisation.

Once Vohne and Kres were settled with Niafe sitting across from them, closer to Vohne than Kres, she began her story.

"Ever since I was little, my mother has been telling me about how she should be the one ruling the kingdom. I used to dream of growing up and becoming queen." Niafe said wistfully.

Kres growled in a manner worthy of a Thresl.

Vohne hid his smile.

She held up a hand in a defensive gesture. "I don't dream of that anymore. I did until I grew old enough to understand my mother is insane. She did something. I don't know what, but she did something to stop the two of you from meeting and triggering the change. There's a man she goes to, a magic user. I think he cast a spell to prevent your last bonding. After all, if you never met your mate, you couldn't change into the king."

"Where is he now?" Vohne asked. He didn't need her to explain to him how he changed. He knew the rules. Vohne had transformed more than any other Thresl in history.

"He died many years ago, which is why I think you were able to come back. His spell blocking your destiny wore off," Niafe explained.

"We need to talk to your mother and find out what he did in case he did the same thing to other Thresls," Kres said, his face set in hard lines.

Vohne didn't like it either, but he didn't want to rush into anything. "We need to think smart. If we rush Lady Nelb, she'll do something even more drastic."

"She already has." Niafe's voice was rushed as if she wanted to get all the words out like ripping off the bandage. "Mother has recruited some soldiers. She plans to take over the castle in three days."

"Why in three days?" Kres asked.

Niafe turned her brilliant eyes to Kres. "Because that's when your marriage ceremony is planned."

Vohne flinched at the glare from his mate's eyes.

"And when were you going to share that happy news?" Kres asked.

Vohne wouldn't have been surprised if icicles formed in the air from the chill in his mate's voice. "Could you give us a moment?" he asked Niafe.

She gave him an innocent smile. "I'll be right out in the hall, bugging your guards."

"It won't take long." Especially if Kres impaled him with his dagger like his eyes were promising he'd do.

Vohne waited to talk until she'd left the room. Once the door shut behind her, he slid to one knee before his lover, his life, his mate. Taking Kres' left hand between his own, he looked up at the one person he adored above all others and always would. "It's tradition for the king to re-marry his mate after each reincarnation. You have been my husband for hundreds of years. Each time you die, I die with you, and when we meet up again, we renew our vows. It's assumed by all that you would be willing to marry me again." He hoped his eyes reflected the deep feelings he had in his heart for this one man. "Were they wrong?"

Kres' handsome face changed from annoyed to confused. "How many times have we gotten married?"

Vohne smiled. His lover hadn't said no. There was still hope. He really didn't want to go in front of his people and tell them that his mate refused his hand in marriage. It would undermine his legitimacy and cause issues later on, but there was no way he was going to bring that up to his mate. He wouldn't pressure him. He'd already taken away all of Kres' other choices in life. He wouldn't take this choice away too. "More times than I care to count," he confessed, mostly because each time they reincarnated, it was because they'd died before.

Kres shifted in his chair but still let Vohne hold onto his hand. "A guy just likes to be asked."

Vohne's head snapped up. His mate's eyes sparkled with amusement. "Would you do me the honour of becoming my husband?"

A teasing smile tilted the edges of Kres' mouth. "Depends on what you're offering. I mean, you have to top the offers from the other guys I have lined up."

"Hmmm, that's tough. You could be the co-ruler of an entire kingdom," he tempted.

Kres shook his head. "I'm not really into that kind of power. I'm a low-key kind of guy."

"Hmm. Riches. I can buy you anything you desire," Vohne offered.

Kres shook his head again. "Money can't buy happiness."

"You're a tough man to please," Vohne said, playing with Kres' fingers as he thought. "How about my undying love and devotion? I can promise I'll never stray, and if I haven't stopped loving you by now, it's never going to happen. Besides, I've already killed all the competition and I'm all you've got left."

Kres laughed. "Well, if you put it that way, I guess I'll have to take you."

Vohne stood up, leaning over his mate. "So you'll marry me?" He didn't want any question in Kres' mind about whether he had agreed to this marriage.

"Yes, I'll marry you."

"Good." Vohne slid his fingers into Kres' hair and pressed their lips together. The familiar flavour of his mate set his body on fire. He wanted to throw Kres on the table and cement their bond, but he knew they needed to talk to Niafe about their plans first. After giving Kres one last kiss, he marched over to the door and ripped it open.

"Come in," he growled to Niafe.

She came back in, and Vohne sat down in the chair beside his mate. Inhaling his mate's calming scent, Vohne gathered his thoughts on how to thwart another uprising.

"Who do you see as my biggest adversaries?" Vohne asked Niafe.

Niafe shifted in her seat, folded her fingers together then set them on her lap. "I don't want you to think badly of me, Your Highness. Going against my family was a difficult decision."

"I understand," Vohne said. A thought occurred to him. "What is your heritage?"

"Half human, half Thresl. My father was human."

"Was?"

"Yes, he died in The Purge. Mother hasn't re-mated."

The silence was filled with the weight of knowledge.

"That's why she's losing her sanity, isn't it?"

Niafe nodded. "It's been a slow slide, but even some of her supporters have urged me to take her place." She gave Vohne a guilty look. "I would never betray you, Your Highness. I believe you were chosen by a higher power, and I support you and your husband's rule."

Kres gave a choking cough.

Vohne kicked him. "Stop it. Whether you want to or not, you're going to rule with me."

"I'm not wearing a crown, and I'm keeping my knife."

Damn, the man was cute when he pouted. "Deal."

Niafe laughed.

He really liked this woman. This would all go better if his brother was there to advise him. A kernel of an idea grew in his mind. If Niafe wasn't mated, maybe she would be a good candidate for Bleine. At least he could introduce them. It would probably be best if he had several potential mates for his brother to choose from. If there was a connection between them, Bleine might not have noticed it while he was bonded with Jallryne. "How well do you know my brother?"

A blush covered Niafe's cheeks. "We've spoken a few times."

"Setting up your brother?" Kres asked.

"Possibly. Niafe, if you were connected to the throne through my brother, do you think your mother would lose her supporters?"

"What?" Kres sat up straight. "She'll have you assassinated and let her daughter take over."

"No." Niafe shook her head. "Not if we sell it to the people that I'm also an advisor. That would buy us time to figure out what to do about my mother. She must be controlled."

"Can she be re-mated?" Vohne wondered if Lady Nelb could be saved if they found her another mate.

"I doubt it." Niafe frowned. "Who would mate with a madwoman?"

"Good point," Vohne agreed.

"Mating with Bleine might work," Niafe said. "I've always thought we had a spark, but as he was bonded, I didn't pursue him."

Vohne turned to look at his mate, who sat quietly beside him, not commenting on the plan.

"What are you planning?"

Kres gave him a sweet smile. "Nothing, dear."

"Uh-huh." Why did his mate's innocent look not reassure him at all?

They spent the next hour discussing how to counteract an invasion, with Niafe filling in the details of her mother's plan.

"My mother will change everything if she finds out I talked to you. You must be prepared for anything. Keep your most trusted men close around you. You and your mate's lives are in danger."

"I've been through this more than once. I know how to quell an uprising. I'll try to save your mother, but make no mistake, if the only way to end this is to kill her, I won't hesitate to do what is right for my people. Having them led by an unbalanced, power-hungry Thresl isn't in anyone's best interests." Vohne didn't want there to be any misunderstanding about his position.

"Understood," Niafe said.

Kres watched the pair interact and wondered what Vohne's brother was like. If he was anything like Kres' mate, Niafe would be a good match.

"Don't you think, love?" Vohne asked.

"Huh?" He'd been so busy watching his lover he hadn't paid attention to what he had said.

Vohne laughed. "You weren't listening, were you?"

Kres shrugged. "I figure you'll tell me anything I need to know, and since I don't know any of the people you're talking about, it doesn't make any sense to me." All he really understood was Lady Nelb needed to die. He could take care of that while Vohne dealt with the intricacies of court life. Kres was a soldier. He saw things more black and white than his surprisingly complex-thinking lover. Who could have known when he first met the man-cat that Vohne would turn out to be a reincarnated king and Kres' soul mate?

"If you paid attention, you would know who your enemies are," Vohne scolded.

"I'm sure he was paying attention," Niafe interjected. Poor girl thought she could head off a fight.

Kres decided to try out their link. *"You can explain it to me later. Use little words and lots of lube,"* he sent telepathically to his mate with what he hoped was a sultry look.

Vohne gave Kres the smile he thought of as his. The one that crinkled his nose and brought out the sparkle in his eyes. Vohne leaned over, pressing a hot, hard kiss on Kres' lips.

"It's a date, my treasure," he said in a low voice.

Niafe cleared her throat, pulling them back to the present.

Time passed in a dull flipping of his knife as papers came out to write down plans and discuss possible enemies.

"I still don't trust Hellbur," Kres commented. "Even if Niafe's mother is behind all this, there's nothing to say Hellbur isn't helping her."

Vohne broke off his conversation with Niafe to face his mate. "True, but I didn't get a sense of deception when I spoke to him."

Kres disagreed. "There's something oily about him. I didn't like how he looked at you."

"Hellbur has always had a crush on the king," Niafe offered.

"How do you know?" Kres asked.

"I read it in a courtier's diary I found in the archives. He apparently wanted to bind your houses years ago, but you turned him down," Niafe replied.

"It's unnatural for two Thresls to match even for a monarchy. I would still need my soul mate, and Kres, even in his mildest incarnation, wouldn't tolerate sharing me."

"True." Kres didn't know what his previous forms had been like. Some of his memories were returning — just in flashes and bits, not enough to form more than a brief idea of what he'd been like before. But he could pretty much guarantee that no incarnation of him would have allowed for sharing. "I can promise if Hellbur wants the same thing now, it's not going to happen."

Vohne laughed. "I'm sure he knows that after meeting you. If not, I'll be happy to inform him."

It was late when the meeting finally finished. They ate a light dinner and went to bed. Their lovemaking was slow and sweet, and when it was over, Kres fell asleep in the arms of the man he loved more than life.

* * * *

Kres awoke to people banging on the door.

"Go away!" he shouted. Blinking, it took him a moment to realise he was alone in bed.

Where the hell had his lover gone?

The door slammed open and a dozen soldiers entered.

"King-Mate, we're here to arrest you for the murder of Lady Nelb," an unfamiliar soldier announced in a voice ringing with authority.

"What?" The sleepy fog clouding his mind blew away, leaving him awake but confused.

Nelrin approached the bed, crouching beside it until they were at eye level. "Your knife was found next to Lady Nelb's body."

"Nonsense, it's right there." Kres pointed towards the bedside table where he'd set it the night before. He sat straight up, staring at the bare spot. "Shit." His knife was gone.

"We don't blame you for killing her. Arresting you is only for show. Please get dressed and come with us," Nelrin said in a soothing tone.

Looking at the guards, he saw that not one of them looked upset over his supposed murder.

"Um, all right." Dressing quickly, he let them lead him away. Now he had to figure out who'd killed Lady Nelb and had framed him for it. The bigger question was where the hell was Vohne?

Kres followed the soldiers, mentally preparing for the rigors of a jail cell. What he wasn't prepared for was the luxurious office he was shown into. Lush carpet sank beneath his booted feet and a soft couch with a wide padded seat dominated the room.

"We thought you'd be more comfortable here, Your Highness," Nelrin said in an apologetic tone, as if expressing regrets for the lack of proper accommodations.

"I'm not the official king-mate yet," Kres reminded him.

"Trust me, after this, you will be more than accepted by the populace," Nelrin said with a smile. "Anyone who had doubts before won't now. You will be seen as the enforcer, the king's right hand."

He watched in astonishment as the soldiers all gave him a respectful salute before leaving the room. Nelrin was the last man out.

"We'll make sure no one bothers you while we wait to find out what the king's reaction will be."

"Don't I get to defend myself?" What kind of bullshit court was Vohne running?

Nelrin shook his head. "Heroes don't need to defend themselves. It will likely be a slap on the wrist or community service. It will be decided by the victim's closest family and confirmed by the king."

Kres was still mulling that over when the soldiers left. Wasn't it convenient that he'd met Niafe last night and her mother had ended up stabbed with his knife? Kres didn't believe in coincidences. Beautiful Niafe was up to her pretty little neck in all this. A neck he imagined throttling when he got out of this place.

Where the hell was his mate? Wasn't he supposed to sense when Kres was upset? Maybe he wasn't worried enough. The entire situation felt unreal, like he was still dreaming—although the calm way the soldiers had brought him here had taken away some of his worries. Plopping down on the comfortable couch, he propped his feet up on the cushioned ottoman and wondered how to prove that Niafe had set him up for murder.

Chapter Nine

Vohne sat at his desk, flipping through the hundredth piece of paperwork. A lot of the information was on the machine on his desk, but the really old stuff was still on paper. He'd sneaked out of their bed early to get some work done, hoping to return to his mate before Kres awoke. Looking at the bright sun outside, he was pretty sure he'd failed.

Rubbing his eyes, he tried to focus on the paper again.

A knock at the door had him lifting his head. "Enter."

Nelrin walked into the room, a wide smile on his face. His mate Friln followed behind.

"We've got your mate in lockdown if you'd like to go see him."

Vohne jumped to his feet. "Why would you arrest Kres?"

"His knife was found by Lady Nelb's body. Lady Niafe demanded we take your king-mate into protective custody. When you weren't in your room with your bonded, we moved his location in case one of Lady Nelb's supporters went looking for him."

"Were anyone else's fingerprints found on the knife?"

Nelrin shrugged. "We didn't bother looking. It's not like it matters anyway. You're not going to have your mate put in the dungeon. Besides, Lady Niafe hates her mother, and I doubt she's even going to press charges. She merely demanded we protect your mate against repercussions, not charge him with anything."

Niafe. For the first time Vohne wondered if maybe he'd had his attention on the wrong family member.

After Nelrin left, Vohne concentrated on his lover. His first instinct was to go free him, but protective custody meant Kres was out of danger. It would do him good to stay put for a bit until Vohne found out what really happened.

"You all right, love?" He sent the question down their shared link. Their bond felt stronger than ever before.

"I hate your planet!"

Vohne laughed. *"Did you kill Lady Nelb?"* He didn't really think Kres had. Not that his lover wasn't capable of murdering anyone — because he was — but more than that, he hadn't had the opportunity. New to the planet, he wouldn't even know where to find Lady Nelb.

"No. But everyone is too busy congratulating me to listen."

"Ahh. Sit tight, love. I'll come check on you in a bit."

"Take your time. I'll let you know before I die of boredom."

"Thank you. I'd appreciate that."

He could feel annoyance more than anything along their connection before he broke off communication. It wouldn't do for him to rush to his lover's defence. If

Kres was going to prove himself as a true king-mate, he needed to take care of his own problems. Vohne would only step in if absolutely necessary. He couldn't let anyone harm his mate, but Kres wasn't made of glass either.

A soft knock at the door drew his attention.

"Enter."

Niafe sauntered into the room, triumph glowing on her face.

Vohne examined her carefully. The woman was dressed as befitted a lady of the court, in sheer layers of locally woven fabric, but the look in her eyes had him shifting uneasily in his seat.

"Good morning, Your Highness. I hear your mate has taken care of our little problem."

Gone was the sincerity of yesterday. The girl who'd reluctantly plotted against her mother and helped him strategise his defence had vanished behind this confident, conniving woman.

"You don't look upset about her death," Vohne said.

Niafe shrugged. "I've lived under my mother's thumb for enough years. This is more of a relief than a moment of mourning."

Vohne propped his elbow on the desk and rested his chin on his hand as he examined her. "Have a seat."

With a brilliant smile, she sat in the chair before his desk.

"Why did you frame my mate for your mother's death?" No point tiptoeing around the fact she had murdered her mother. Vohne had no doubt in his mind she'd done the deed.

Niafe's jaw dropped open for a second, but she quickly recovered. "Why would you think I killed my mother?"

Vohne stared at her for a long moment — waiting.

Niafe jumped to her feet. "Fine! You want to hear that I killed the psychopath who tried to ruin my life and unbalance the monarchy? Then you're right." She pointed a finger towards the door. "But everyone thinks your mate is a hero. He can ride this out with the backing of the entire kingdom in his pocket. Do you think they'd do the same thing with a woman who kills her own mother?"

"Perhaps not, but how can I trust you with my brother if you don't think anything about framing my love?" Her deception bothered Vohne more than anything. If she could easily dispose of her mother, what would she do when Bleine became inconvenient?

"You forget one thing, Your Highness. I don't need your permission to bond with your brother. I just need your brother's. Hell, we might not even be mates, but I was willing to bet my mother's life on it." With a cold look at Vohne, she stormed out of the room.

Vohne shook his head at her exit. She'd killed her own mother and still thought she had a chance with Bleine. Unfortunately for her, there were two major flaws in her plan. First, Bleine's intelligence rated even higher than Vohne's, and he would let himself die before being used by another woman. Secondly, Vohne didn't plan on bringing his brother out of deep freeze until he had a viable candidate. If Niafe thought she could blackmail Vohne into a mating with his brother, she wasn't as smart as she thought.

Vohne sat at his desk for a bit, wrapping up some more paperwork before deciding it was time to go check on his lover. Kres might get into trouble if left too long on his own. Hell, he might have already left wherever they'd had him stashed, guards or no guards.

Ignoring the soldiers who fell in step behind him, Vohne headed towards where he could feel his mate biding his time.

As he approached, the door guards snapped to attention.

"Has he been behaving?" Vohne asked.

"Yes, Your Highness," they replied in unison.

"Hmm." Vohne opened the door and stepped inside. Three steps into the room, he was jumped. Air burst from his chest as he fell onto the soft carpet, a familiar hard body pressing against him.

"Took you long enough to check on me." Kres' hot breath brushed across his ear. "Now that I have you, whatever am I going to do with you, hmmm?"

"Problem, Your Highness?" one of the soldiers asked. Vohne could hear the amusement in the soldier's voice.

"Nothing I can't handle," he replied.

With a quick flick of his muscles, he spun around and pinned his laughing mate to the carpet.

"What are you going to do now?" he teased.

Kres relaxed completely beneath his hold, his eyes sparkling with laughter.

"I guess I'll have to give in to your obvious superiority," he said, rubbing his body against Vohne's like a cat in heat.

Vohne looked up to the men in the doorway. "Leave us."

With knowing chuckles, the guards left, closing the door gently behind them.

Kres moved beneath Vohne, his body hot, hard and delicious—perfect.

"Mmm." Vohne leant down to taste his lover. Kres turned his head.

Vohne growled. "What is that for?"

A smirk crossed his mate's lips. "You think because you have me trapped, I'm just going to give it up?"

"You're not?" Vohne knew a bit of desperation coloured his tone, but he needed to feel Kres around him.

"Nope." Kres licked his lips, taunting Vohne with their slickness. "Like all good things, you need to fight for what you want."

Vohne had foolishly relaxed against his lover during their chat. Before he knew it, Kres had flipped him onto his back, sliding on top and pinning Vohne to the floor by his wrists.

"Gotcha," his victorious mate announced.

Vohne couldn't hold back his grin. "I guess I'm just a prisoner to your whims."

Kres frowned at him suspiciously. "I fell into your trap, didn't I?"

"Never try to out-strategise a king, my love," Vohne teased.

Sighing, Kres gave him a hot, hard kiss. "I guess I'll just have to fuck you until you can't be so sneaky."

"Good plan," Vohne agreed. Of course he didn't tell his mate that he would agree to about anything if it involved his hard, muscular body naked and against Vohne. No need to give the man the total advantage. He knew from experience the difficulty in resisting his mate's charms during a disagreement. Luckily, this one time they were in perfect accord. "I don't suppose we can move this to the couch so I don't get rug burns?"

Kres smiled. "Nope. It will remind you later about the dangers of trying to outsmart your mate."

Vohne laughed. "Yep, that will teach me."

Kres dipped his head to taste the flavour of his lover. Just as he was enjoying the feel of his hot mate beneath him, a blaring alarm ripped through their warm cocoon.

Before he could figure out where the alarm was coming from, Vohne quickly rolled them until he was on top. He jumped to his feet and offered Kres his hand.

"What's going on?"

"That bitch must've tripped the thawer. She's going to try to bring back my brother before I can warn him."

"What bitch?"

"Niafe. She came to me earlier and confessed to killing her mother. Tried to tell me she was doing you a favour, building up your reputation."

"I'm not sure that's a reputation I want to have," Kres replied.

Vohne wrapped a hand around Kres' arm, pulling him towards the door. "We've got to stop her. Bleine will be disorientated when he first comes back. He might not be able to see through her bullshit. Here."

Kres instinctively grabbed the handle of the dagger his lover handed to him. "What's this?"

"To replace your lost one," Vohne said.

"Aw, that's sweet. Most men bring flowers."

Vohne gave a bark of laughter. "Let's go before my brother is taken advantage of."

Kres walked fast to keep up with his lover. "But won't he be…um…be unable to perform? I mean, if my danglies get frozen they aren't going to work."

Vohne gave Kres a quick kiss on the cheek as they walked, proving the man had amazing coordination. "Thresls have amazing recuperative powers."

"I have noticed that." Kres hurried to keep up with Vohne as the stronger man yanked him along.

Ripping open the door, Vohne glared at the soldiers. "Why are you still here? Niafe is after my brother. I want her stopped before my brother regains consciousness."

The guards ran down the hall towards the alarm.

"Idiots," Vohne muttered.

He still didn't let go of Kres as they followed the soldiers.

"Why aren't we running?"

"Kings don't run."

"Really?" Kres wondered if that really was true or if Vohne was feeding him lies.

"Unless our mates are involved." Vohne flashed him a hot smile. "I'd run anywhere for you."

After what felt like an endless stream of hallways, they reached a point where a dozen soldiers stood outside a metal door.

"What's going on?"

Kres' hormones stood at attention at the forceful tone of his lover. Hot images of his lover using that commanding voice in the bedroom made him harder than the solid door before him. Pulling his shirt down farther, he futilely tried to hide his erection. Luckily all eyes were on Vohne and ignoring Kres for the moment.

Nelrin came forward, bowing low before the king. "She's locked the door, overriding the security measures."

Kres' blood ran cold. If she blocked them long enough, she could thaw out Vohne's brother and cause all kinds of trouble. He couldn't let her get to Bleine. His mate loved his brother, and it would break

Vohne's heart if Bleine re-mated with this scheming bitch.

No one was allowed to upset his mate!

Kres scanned the doorframe and the electronic panel caught his eye. "Can't you override the system?"

Vohne shook his head. "Security has changed since I was here last. They didn't even have electric locks."

"Huh."

Kres walked up to the security panel and plunged his knife into the interface with all his force. A popping noise sounded, followed by the smell of burnt electronics polluting the air. The doors slid apart.

Vohne flashed him a look of admiration. "Good thinking."

Kres shrugged. "Sometimes the direct approach is best."

The guards rushed in ahead of them. A moment later, the sounds of a struggle and shouting reached their ears.

Yanking his knife out of the wall, Kres retained hold of his mate as they entered the room. It was eerie as fuck to see walls of people hanging from metal tubes filled with blue goo and bodies.

"Who are all these people?" His voice was barely a whisper. He didn't want Niafe to hear him, and truthfully, the room creeped him out. He nervously gripped the knife tighter as they approached.

"Most of them lost their mate or have severe illness or injury and are waiting to be cured. Some will be here for a brief while, others centuries," Vohne explained in an equally quiet voice.

Chills prickled Kres' skin as he moved with Vohne through the room. Several tubes hung from hooks in the middle of the room like something out of a horror movie. "It's kind of disturbing."

Vohne gave a soft laugh. Kres hoped there never came a time where Vohne needed to be cryogenically frozen. He didn't know if he could do it.

"I demand to see the king!" Niafe's shrieking voice echoed throughout the chamber.

"I believe that's our cue." Vohne yanked free of Kres' hold and walked quickly towards the sound.

"Shit." Kres rushed after him, determined to protect Vohne by any means necessary.

He skidded to a halt when they reached the area where Niafe stood, held between two guards beside Bleine's cryo tube.

"Why are you doing this?" she asked Vohne. Kres had to give her credit. With her attitude, she made the guards seem more like accessories than the people who held her captive. Despite being a psycho, the girl had style.

"You've admitted to murdering your mother and framing my mate. Now you think I'm going to let you bond with my brother?" Vohne asked, his voice revealing his astonishment.

"I deserve this!" For the first time Kres saw cracks in her composure. "I deserve to be queen." Madness lived in her eyes.

"You're the reason we didn't meet last time, aren't you? It wasn't your mother at all," Kres demanded.

She turned imploring eyes to Kres, like he was going to side with her, as if she were only misunderstood instead of crazy. He had missed her deceit because she hadn't thought she was fooling him. She truly believed she was fulfilling her personal prophecy. "It's Mother's fault he came back this time. I had it all under control, but no, she said it was unnatural to deprive the people of their king. I think it's unnatural to deprive people of a bloodline. I can bring new blood and children to the throne. Instead of recycling the same garbage, we could have a fresh start. With enough human blood in our system, we won't need full humans."

"I am imprisoning you as an enemy of the crown." Vohne's voice remained calm and even, but Kres could feel fury pulsing through their link.

"You can lock me up, but you can never stop us all. We will take back this planet from antiquated ideas and bring it into the future," Niafe shrieked.

Kres stepped forward. "We will stop you all. Anyone who threatens my man won't have to worry about jail." He let the threat hang in the air.

She softened her stance as she looked at him. "Kres, we can be friends. I don't blame you for following your mate's lead. You've been doing it for so long you don't know any better. Join with me and I can free you from his influence. As the acknowledged king-mate, you and I can rule together."

Kres couldn't believe the woman's gall. "You don't care who rules by your side as long as you can rule. I don't know who you have behind you, but they'd best watch for that knife in their back."

"I could make you king!" she screamed.

Shaking his head, Kres gave her a pitying look. "Honey, that's where you made your mistake. I've never wanted to be king."

With a shriek of fury, she shoved free of her guards. "If I can't have him, neither can you." With inhuman strength, she kicked Bleine's chamber.

Before their horrified gaze, the cryogenic pod fell over, the glass face plate shattering on the floor.

"No!" Vohne rushed to his brother's side. Bleine's body convulsed from the shock of sudden exposure.

"Get the medic!" Kres shouted. "And contain her." He didn't know what stood as a doctor on this planet, but if they didn't get help soon, his mate's brother wouldn't survive.

Vohne opened the tube, revealing Bleine gasping for air.

The sound of someone choking drew Kres' attention to his right.

A soldier lay curled up and shivering on the floor. "What's wrong with him?" he asked the closest soldier.

The man rushed over to hold down the shaking man. "Sarler is an empath."

"Human?" Kres asked.

"Yeah."

"Perfect."

Kres lifted the slim human in his arms. Luckily, the guy was fairly light. He might be a soldier, but Kres wasn't up to Thresl strength.

He almost dropped Sarler twice on the way over to Bleine. The kid kept wiggling and convulsing.

Vohne looked up. "What are you doing?"

"I'm solving this problem. The medics are taking too long."

Kres carefully laid the empath beside Bleine then pressed the men's hands together.

Immediately, the convulsions stopped. Bleine's eyes snapped open, the focus in them sharp as if he'd just closed them instead of having been in a cryogenic chamber. Sitting up, he leaned over the empath and planted a kiss on the young human.

Pleased with his solution, Kres stepped back and found himself the focus of his mate's disapproving look.

"What?"

"Bleine isn't gay."

He looked down at the two men kissing then back at Vohne. "Looks like he's doing fine to me. Want me to give him some pointers?"

"No! He is mine. I'll kill you!" Niafe's voice cut through the room.

Kres looked over in time to see Niafe slide a knife out of her boot and stab one of the distracted guards. The second guard grabbed at her as she ran for Bleine.

Instinct took over.

Snatching up his weapon, Kres threw it at her. The blade spun in the air with a soft whistling noise before embedding in the centre of her throat.

With a strangled gasp, Niafe fell to the ground, fingers scrabbling at the dagger. Before she could pull it out, her movements stilled. Blood poured from the wound, and her eyes rolled to the back of her head.

Kres was sick of people trying to kill him. Damn it, he'd come here to have a peaceful life with his lover, and he was going to have peace if he had to stab every one of the fuckers.

A medic shoved through the crowd, falling to his knees beside her.

"About time you got here," Kres growled. "She's dead. Check the prince."

The man paled beneath Kres' glare. With shaking hands, he pulled an instrument out of his bag then waved a long glowing wand over the two men. "Prince Bleine and his mate will be fine." He pulled a syringe out of his bag then quickly injected Bleine. "This will help his body adapt."

The human tore himself away from Bleine. "I can't be his mate."

"Why not?" Bleine asked.

"Neither of us are lovers of men."

Kres shook his head. "You people are too much drama for me. I'm going to bed. I've had a long day." Turning on his heel, he marched out of the room.

He hid his smile as he heard Vohne's footsteps follow him. He'd know the sound of his mate anywhere.

"Would you like company?"

He gave his mate a careful once-over. "You might as well come along and pound me into the mattress. I mean, other than ruling a planet, you've got nothing to do."

Vohne gave a choked laugh. "True."

"Maybe we should get you a hobby, like flower arranging," Kres said, warming to his theme.

"Why would I need to arrange flowers?"

Kres flashed him an innocent look. "Well, they're not going to arrange themselves."

"True. Or I could just be your boy toy," Vohne offered.

"Hmmm." Kres gave the idea the serious attention the proposal deserved. "You're certainly pretty enough, but can you practise saying important things like yes, sir, whatever you say, sir? Because I really get off on the power thing."

Vohne's rich laugh filled the corridor. "Yes, I've heard you're a power hungry bastard."

"Yep, that's me." Switching thoughts, he turned serious. "We'll need to figure out who Niafe was working with."

Vohne nodded. "But not today. Today we'll enjoy each other. We'll have time after our mating ceremony to hunt down the betrayers."

"Maybe your brother will have better insight."

"Maybe," Vohne agreed.

"I think that was supposed to be maybe, *sir*." Reaching over, Kres pinched Vohne's ass before fleeing down the hall, laughing as he heard his mate chasing after him. So much for kings never running.

Tonight, they would enjoy their bond. Tomorrow, he had to be fitted with formal robes for the mating ceremony and do the million and one things a king-mate was required to do. Glancing back at his quickly gaining lover, he decided, despite all the drama, he would do anything for the man-cat he loved.

PRINCE CLAIMED

Dedication

To my sci-fi fans, who didn't laugh when I created a
species of futuristic cat people.

Chapter One

Bleine bit his lip to hold back a shout as his orgasm tore through him. Cum splattered across the sheets and dripped down his fist in long, sticky strands as the stench of sex filled the room without the happy afterglow of a partner to cuddle with afterwards.

While gulping in air in fast desperate breaths, Bleine blinked to clear his vision. He grabbed for the box of tissues he now kept on his bedside table. His nightly releases had ruined more than one washcloth so he'd moved on to disposables. Tendrils of dream memories wafted through his mind. Bleine licked his lips, trying to recapture the lingering, imaginary taste of his mate. The sweet flavour of honey still coated his tongue as if he'd just kissed his mate Sarler after eating a sticky bun. His heart, empty and aching, beat sluggishly as the hollow feeling expanded to wrap him completely in despair. Without his bonded, it was almost as if he'd ceased to exist and wandered as a shadowy figure in his own life.

A peek at the wall clock revealed it was still several hours before morning. He wondered if Sarler was sleeping well. The process of bonding to mates went easier when going from Thresl to human form. Since Bleine had been human when he'd met his bonded, the process of joining souls had taken longer. It might take forever if he couldn't coax Sarler to stay the night in his bed. Three days had passed since they'd bonded and already he could feel his mind beginning to unravel. If they didn't have sex soon, without a human to anchor him, Bleine would descend into madness. No one knew how close he skated to losing his identity. He wouldn't pressure Sarler into a deeper bond or reveal his troubles to his brother.

Vohne had enough issues trying to arrange a bonding ceremony with his fractious mate. Already they'd pushed back the wedding a month in order to get everything together and allow time for guests to arrive from around and outside the galaxy. A coveted invitation to the Thresl king's wedding could make a political career, so invitees had to be chosen with care.

During his waking hours, Bleine spent his time focused on finding the betrayers — the group of people plotting against his brother, the king. Only when sleeping did images of Sarler haunt him. Beautiful Sarler. With his pale hair and sweet grey eyes, he reminded Bleine of the picture of a wood sprite he'd seen in a storybook as a child. His mother had used to read to him stories of forest dwellers who bonded with the wildlife and lived in peace. He'd been enchanted with the idea as a boy and had often searched for sprites when he had gone camping.

He'd never found one, of course. Sarler was the closest he'd ever come. Unfortunately, he was having as much luck capturing him as he had done catching a forest sprite as a child.

"Fuck!" he growled. Discontent radiated through him. He wanted to wake up beside Sarler, not all alone with no one for company but his own hand.

Damn Kreslan.

Bleine sighed. As much as he wanted to blame his brother's mate, he couldn't. If Kreslan hadn't interfered... Hell, he'd be dead. Kres had saved Bleine's life by finding him a bondmate as soon as Bleine had broken free from the cryo-pod. The scheming bitch who'd shattered his tube hadn't counted on Kres' quick action to find him a fast replacement.

Fortunately, unlike his brother, Bleine could re-bond. If Kres died, Vohne would quickly follow. A cryo-chamber couldn't save the king if his one and only mate lost his life. The same as hundreds of years before, Kres and Vohne would reincarnate together.

One advantage to not being the true king was that Bleine's mates didn't reincarnate. Sadly, it also led to him choosing the wrong people to bond with. Unlike Vohne, Bleine's choices weren't fated to be his perfect match. His first bonded had died in the Great Purge, killed by a fanatic while Bleine had been out fighting. His second bonded had tried to kill Vohne...and now his third didn't want him. So far, his record hadn't been stellar.

Sarler, his current bonded, was actively avoiding Bleine.

He didn't know what to do to get his bondmate's attention. Even though his patience was failing, becoming a stalker wasn't on his 'to do' list.

The fact that Sarler had never had sex with a male added to their complications. Although Bleine had always bonded with females, the Thresls as a species didn't discriminate between male and female partners.

They chose the person, not their sex. Bleine worried that Sarler didn't have the same outlook. Humans sometimes weren't as flexible with their sexuality. If Sarler fixated on Bleine being a male instead of a preferred female, they wouldn't ever become closer.

He didn't know if it was because he had bonded with an empath, but Bleine woke up every morning coated with his own spunk and aching for the touch of someone he barely knew. He had hoped that Sarler's empathic powers might make it harder for him to resist the bond, to resist Bleine. So far that hadn't proved to be the case.

The compulsion to touch, cuddle and keep Sarler from all harm rode Bleine like a driving force, until he wished to go to the counselling centre and snatch his mate from the presence of others. Sarler worked as an empath for those coming into the cryogenic centre, helping them with the transition either from or to the chambers and monitoring their condition once frozen. After the Great Purge, hundreds of Thresls had to be put in cryo-chambers to retain their sanity after their mates had been slaughtered.

The emotional trauma experienced when coming out of a frozen environment could be overpowering for some, and not everyone survived. When Bleine had been abruptly jerked out of hibernation, Kres' quick action that day had saved Bleine from going into shock from lack of a soul partner. Any Thresl who had already converted and lost their mate could die or go mad from lack of the bond that kept Thresls in their final form.

It didn't make it any easier that now, although bonded, Bleine continued to wake up alone because his mate wasn't into men. The kiss they'd shared at their initial pairing had seared through Bleine, hotter than his previous full sex encounters with the female bondmates he'd had before.

He would do just about anything to taste Sarler's mouth again. To feel Sarler's body against his and their lips sliding together in a combustible combination of want and need.

A knock on his door pulled Bleine away from his morose thoughts.

Curious about who could be visiting in the middle of the night, he slid on a pair of sleep pants and rushed to answer it. People never came to deliver good news at two in the morning. After yanking the door open, he stopped and stared, unable to think of a single word.

Sarler stood in his doorway, his blond hair sticking out on all sides. He glared with red-rimmed eyes at Bleine as if he'd done something horribly wrong. He wore red pyjama bottoms, a thin white shirt and no shoes.

"What's up?" He tried to sound casual while his heart increased its usual rhythm and his cock tried valiantly to harden again.

Sarler shoved Bleine aside then stomped past him into Bleine's suite.

Confused, Bleine closed the door. He leaned against the firm wood surface, needing the extra support for whatever news his mate had come to share.

Sarler opened his mouth a few times only to close it again without saying anything.

"Are you okay?" Bleine asked tentatively. He tried to keep his tone neutral. Though Bleine was glad to see his bondmate, Sarler had a skittish twitch about him and Bleine didn't want to scare him off.

Sarler's expression didn't appear welcoming to Bleine as he ran a hand through his hair and began to pace. Bleine kept still, not wanting to interrupt whatever thoughts were spinning through Sarler's head until his mate was ready to share them. He'd learnt patience in his years of rule. Moments of importance couldn't be rushed.

Finally the words burst out of Sarler like heavy rain, frantic and pounding. "I can't sleep. I can barely eat. I think about you every minute of every day." Sarler spun around and pointed at Bleine. "You need to stay out of my head. And please, by the gods, *please* stop touching yourself! I wake up every morning with this!"

Sarler pointed to his crotch. His large erection stood out in sharp relief against the front of his sleep pants. Bleine's mouth watered. He knew exactly how to help with that particular problem. Hell, he even had some movies he'd be happy to share. The past few days he'd been a good researcher and had done his homework.

"I'd be glad to help you with that," Bleine offered. Images flashed through his head. Pictures of Sarler's face as Bleine sucked him off, the beauty of Sarler's expression when Bleine brought him to completion. Oh, yes, he had plenty of ideas.

"Stop it!" Sarler said through gritted teeth. He blushed, turning his pale skin redder than a jungle blood flower. Bleine smiled, entranced by the beautiful colour on his mate's cheeks.

"I–I've never been with a man. That isn't allowed on my planet," Sarler replied. His shaky tone revealed his nerves were even jitterier than Bleine's.

"That's all right," Bleine said. "We aren't on your planet. Anything is allowed here between consenting adults."

Sarler licked his lips, drawing Bleine's attention to the wet slick left behind. The urge to taste Sarler's soft looking mouth struck him like a fist to the gut.

He made a soft noise of need, barely vocal.

"That's what I'm talking about. Stop that." Sarler's eyes flashed with temper and heat. His expression did nothing to cool Bleine's ardour.

Bleine closed his eyes to block out the sight of his mate before he did something unwise, like jumping him. "I can't. You're my bonded."

He could hear the desperation in his voice but could do nothing to stop it. If Sarler didn't even welcome his touch, they were going to have the shortest mating in history. Bleine didn't look forward to returning to the cryogenic chamber, but he wouldn't bond an unwilling person to him for life. Whether his brother would agree to let him go was an entirely different matter.

"What are we going to do?" Confusion caused a sharp crease in Sarler's forehead. "We can't go on this way. I need rest. I can barely function. Images of you fill my head all the fucking time."

The curse coming out of Sarler's soft mouth and spoken in his gentle voice made Bleine smile. Some people couldn't swear effectively. It pleased him that his mate appeared to be one of them.

"Come." Bleine straightened from his spot against the door and held out his hand.

Sarler examined Bleine for a long minute, not moving from his spot. Bleine waited. No point in rushing when he was so close to getting his wish. Eventually—cautiously—Sarler slid his hand into Bleine's.

"Let's get some sleep," Bleine said. There was so much more he'd like to do to his bonded, but sleeping together, building a link between them, ranked higher in importance than having sex despite what his needy body tried to tell him.

"Okay." Sarler smiled at Bleine. A small smile but a good sign overall. Without another word in case he frightened off his nervous mate, Bleine lead Sarler to the bedroom.

Once they were through the door, Bleine released Sarler's hand then crawled onto the bed and between the sheets. He scooted all the way to the side to make room for Sarler. With only a brief hesitation, Sarler climbed in beside Bleine.

"Take off your shirt," Bleine ordered.

"I don't..." Sarler gave him a hesitant look as if unsure of what to do about his demand.

"Now! We need contact to soothe the nervous energy between us. As a counsellor you should know skin-to-skin contact is the best." Bleine needed to feel Sarler's flesh against his own. To calm the craving for his mate's touch. If he had to make it an official command, he would. Being a prince had a few benefits.

Sarler yanked off his top, exposing a smooth line of skin and muscle. Frowning his displeasure, he asked, "What about my pants?"

Bleine looked at the pyjama bottoms. "You can keep them on if you want to." He wanted to insist that Sarler strip completely, but pushing his luck at this point could be more detrimental than the benefits of having a naked cuddle with his mate.

To Bleine's disappointment, Sarler remained half dressed.

Holding back a sigh, Bleine lifted the covers. Sarler slid all the way to Bleine's side before turning to face away from him.

Not willing to miss an opportunity to snuggle his mate, Bleine wrapped an arm around Sarler. Strong, sinewy muscles moved beneath his palm and a deep purr rolled up his throat. Sarler's physique didn't resemble Bleine's larger body at all. A round mole on his mate's shoulder caught Bleine's attention. Unable to resist, he placed a soft kiss on the mark.

"What are you doing?" Sarler asked, stiffening in Bleine's arms.

"Sorry. Your beauty spot needed kissing," Bleine replied. There was only so much control one man could be expected to have.

"Oh." Sarler relaxed in Bleine's hold as if calmed by his explanation.

Bleine stayed awake for hours watching Sarler sleep until eventually Sarler's slow, even breathing soothed him into closing his eyes.

* * * *

Soft kisses woke Bleine, landing on his cheeks, his chin and that special spot behind his ear that made him purr. Bleine sighed as a warm wave of contentment washed over him like pools of sunshine. He didn't want to open his eyes. If he did, Sarler might stop kissing him. He tilted his head up, offering his neck for more kisses.

"I know you're awake," Sarler whispered in his ear.

Bleine slowly opened his eyes, hoping to prolong the perfect moment. "I didn't want to discourage you."

Waking up to Sarler's attentions? Better than any dream. He'd do anything he could to encourage more touching. His Thresl nature made him want to conform to please his mate. If Sarler had found Bleine in his animal form, he might have become female instead of male. However, now that he'd already been created, changes could only occur internally. His personality would gradually transform over time to become the one most suited to his bonded, but physically he would always remain as he was now.

Hopefully, Sarler would come to appreciate the Thresl he had got. Bleine needed to do whatever he could to keep Sarler's attention. He couldn't risk another bonding. He just couldn't. The trauma of matching up with a human shouldn't be done more than once. The fact that he had survived a third connection had palace gossips wagging that perhaps he had used forbidden magic to make his bonding stick.

Vohne had put most of those rumours to rest and talk had ceased for the moment, but even the king couldn't protect Bleine from sly looks and considering stares.

Sarler leaned over him, a smile curving his lips. The sight of his mate so close pulled Bleine's mind from his unpleasant thoughts. How could he dwell on the negative with this beautiful man above him?

"Good morning," Bleine said. His voice sounded rough. He sat up and poured a glass of water from the pitcher by his bed.

Tipping his head, he offered Sarler a drink.

"No, thank you," Sarler replied, more polite than a half-naked man in Bleine's bed should be.

Bleine tried to keep it casual, but his morning erection brushed against Sarler's thigh when he turned back around.

Bleine drank the liquid greedily, his mind racing to figure out what to say, how to ask if Sarler had changed his mind about wanting Bleine. Sarler had never come right out and denied Bleine, but he hadn't exactly rushed into his arms before last night, and that had been more out of desperation than desire. Lack of sleep could make anyone do things they would normally avoid. Bleine didn't want to read too much into it, or into the kisses he'd received.

"Did you sleep well?" he asked.

"Better than I have in days," Sarler admitted. Wary grey eyes examined Bleine as if waiting for him to boot Sarler out of bed. As far as Bleine was concerned Sarler could stay there until the end of time. He'd happily get bedsores while snuggling forever with his mate.

Vohne and Kres would probably have to come and kick their asses out before Bleine left voluntarily. Setting his glass down, Bleine continued to search for the right words. For a prince who had been taught diplomacy at his father's knee, all his smooth words had deserted him. He'd never done well with voicing his feelings to those closest to him. Give him a dinner with a viper-tongued lord or lady and he'd be fine. Right now he'd almost prefer that. The lust and longing glowing in Sarler's eyes demanded Bleine say something profound or useful or anything at all to ease the growing tension between them.

The words stuck in Bleine's throat. He wanted to demand more — insist on more — but he had to put his bonded mate's needs above his own. He couldn't rush him. "I know you aren't sure about this bonding thing, but if you want to sleep here every night it would at least help you function during the day."

He held his breath as he waited for Sarler's answer.

Sarler nodded. "I'd like that."

He traced Bleine's mouth with the tips of his fingers. Bleine waited for further words, but after a moment he realised none were forthcoming. Maybe talking was overrated. The light touching, maddening and compelling, drove him insane. He fought the compulsion to roll over and pin Sarler's slimmer frame beneath him. His muscles ached as he tensed his body to resist the urge.

"I can feel your anxiety, your need," Sarler explained. "It burns through my body like an insatiable itch I can't scratch. Only you can scratch it."

Bleine could think of all kinds of places he'd like to scratch, but he didn't want to scare away his mate. As much as Sarler talked about feeling Bleine's desire, he hadn't voiced any of his own. Before he touched Sarler sexually, Bleine needed to know the passion was two-sided. He didn't want Sarler to later think that Bleine had pressured him into anything.

"Sorry," Bleine offered. He didn't know what else to say. He couldn't stop the nerves swirling like a dust devil through his body, or the dragon fire of want burning through his veins. Craving his mate was a natural Thresl response to a bonding.

"Don't be sorry," Sarler said. "I decided last night to give us a try. We can either curse our connection for the rest of our lives or cherish it. Besides, you're a beautiful man. If I were going to choose a male, you would be on the top of my list." A shy smile crossed Sarler's face.

"Can you overlook the fact I'm a man? That seemed like a big deal to you." Bleine barely breathed as he waited for Sarler's answer.

Sarler sighed. "I know. I'm still concerned about it. On my world, I would be put to death for daring to enter a same sex contract. But like you said, I don't live there anymore and we're going to be together a long time. Denying our connection only hurts us both. I'm willing to work on our relationship if you are."

Bleine narrowed his eyes at his mate. Although Sarler appeared sincere, the fast change in perspectives had Bleine worried. "Why the quick about-face? Last night you were almost hysterical from feeling my desire."

"I was tired." Sarler brushed it off. "I haven't slept since we bonded. I needed rest. I'm an empath, Bleine. I could feel you even when we weren't in the same room. Besides, if you need me that much I can't let you suffer. I know what happens to Thresls who don't bond."

Bleine stiffened. His stomach swirled like a whirlpool while a tension headache clawed at his brain. This wasn't what he wanted, Sarler to sacrifice himself for the good of the Thresl. He'd die before he accepted a mate who pitied him.

Swallowing back his nausea, Bleine set the record straight. "I held a world together for a hundred years during the Great Purge while waiting for my brother to return. I've survived the death of two bondmates and being cryogenically frozen. I might want you but I don't need a pity fuck," Bleine snarled.

He slid out of bed then headed for the shower. He refused to have a mate out of a sense of duty, or mercy, or whatever story Sarler told himself to make it all right in his mind to mate with Bleine.

Bleine had lived a long life and if he needed to end it now, he'd happily sacrifice himself for his people. They had their king back—they didn't really need him anymore. He'd rather be dead than have a bondmate unable to love him. He'd had that with Jallryne. He'd always suspected she had bonded with him for the power, but at least she'd wanted him for something, even if she'd had to die in the end. He didn't have anything Sarler wanted and he refused to be pitied. It was an honour to bond with a Thresl, not a burden.

He hoped by the time he finished his shower that Sarler would have taken the hint and left.

Chapter Two

Sarler sighed. He blinked back tears as he realised what a huge, bad mistake he'd just made. Looking around the beautiful suite, he felt lower than a two inch Tarkadi worm.

He'd tried to put a positive spin on their situation, never thinking Bleine would take it as an insult. Sarler sat up in bed, uncomfortable now with remaining lying down after he'd ruined everything. Not ever having had a male partner and not *wanting* one weren't the same thing. One of the reasons he'd left his rigidly moral home world was because they didn't approve of same sex pairings. Sex was for procreation only in their minds. Pleasure was frowned upon.

Sarler hoped Bleine would give him another chance. So far the prince had been more than patient with Sarler, letting him take all the time he needed to get his head on straight and figure out what to do.

"He has to. He could die," Sarler whispered to the empty room. Bonding with a Thresl wasn't like gaining a temporary lover. Thresls committed for life. Theirs. As it was, Bleine would have been well within his rights to demand Sarler stay at his suite and in his bed. Not only was he a prince, but Thresls were given a lot of leeway when it came to handling their bonded. If Bleine had tossed Sarler over his shoulder and dragged him off to his room, no one would've lifted a hand.

Instead, Bleine had let Sarler come to him—and what had he done? Blown the entire thing. He'd hoped by waking the prince with kisses he would have conveyed his interest in pursuing their bond. Instead, he'd convinced Bleine that he'd talked himself into being a Thresl mate.

"I'm an idiot," he whispered to the empty room.

His heart ached with the emotional pain pouring from the bathroom. He might as well have taken a knife and filleted the prince to spare him the agony of being unwanted. It would've been kinder.

The problem was, he *did* like the prince. Unfortunately, being an empath didn't make him any less socially awkward. Knowing a person's emotions didn't always lead to better understanding. Prince Bleine's complex personality made him harder to read than most and unfortunately it didn't look as if being the prince's bonded gave Sarler any additional insight into the man.

Most people imagined once you bonded with a Thresl, all your relationship issues were over. Sadly, they didn't understand that, although a Thresl couldn't leave his or her mate without tragic consequences, it didn't mean problems or misunderstandings didn't occur. Fights were sometimes worse when you couldn't leave. Even when meeting happy couples, sometimes Sarler could spot tiny fractures in their bond, pieces that didn't quite fit. Only the royal couple of the king and his mate were perfectly meshed together. They might fight — quite publicly sometimes — but there was never any true heat to their actions. Love flared between them strong enough that Sarler sometimes got an empathic high simply from being in their presence. He wanted the same with his mate. Now he had to try to figure out how to fix the mess he'd caused.

The water continued to run and Sarler knew Bleine was stalling. Probably hoping that when he returned Sarler would be gone.

"I'm leaving," Sarler murmured. Even with his Thresl hearing, Bleine wouldn't have heard him, but it had still felt good to say it.

They both needed some time to regroup. Sarler crawled out of bed, pulled on his shirt then ran his fingers through his hair. The prince deserved some time alone and Sarler needed to get to work. Maybe he could talk to the king-mate about Bleine later. If nothing else Kreslan owed Sarler a few minutes of advice for bonding him to Bleine without his permission anyway.

Having resolved to talk to Kreslan as soon as he got the chance, Sarler left Bleine's suite.

He nodded to the prince's bodyguards as he left. He didn't know their names and didn't care to learn them right now anyway, but they'd been kind enough to let him pass despite his agitated state last night.

A quick stop at his small room for a shower and change of clothes had him ready for the day. Finally refreshed from hours of rest after nights of not sleeping, Sarler walked to the lab with a lighter step. He might need to work details out with Bleine, but the prince couldn't deny him when he came over tonight to sleep. Maybe tonight he could try to convey with his body his willingness that he wasn't smart enough to state with words.

Maybe he'd be brave enough to take off all his clothes this time. Surely Bleine wouldn't be able to resist? Various scenarios of planning a seductive trap for his handsome prince danced through Bleine's mind. Caught in his own thoughts, he didn't pay attention to where he was walking. Turning the corner, he slammed into a hard body. He gasped as he stumbled back and realised he'd walked into the king.

"I'm sorry, your highness." Sarler gave an awkward, hurried bow. King Vohne stood several impressive inches taller than Sarler's smaller frame and he had the presence of someone three times the size.

"No need for that. We're family," King Vohne said. He frowned at Sarler. "Is something wrong?"

"Your brother hates me," Sarler replied sadly.

Vohne gave Sarler a sympathetic smile. He could feel the king's compassion rolling over him in long, soothing waves, wrapping around him in comfort. If Sarler were Thresl he would've purred.

"I doubt he hates you. Bleine dislikes few people. He tries to find the good in everyone," Vohne reassured him.

Sarler couldn't hold back the sigh. Vohne didn't know how badly he'd screwed things up, so he could be excused for his optimism. "Trust me, I'm the exception."

"Want to talk about it?" Vohne asked apparently prepared to lend an ear to the poor sap bonded with his brother.

The king's invitation to discuss Bleine tugged at Sarler, but right now he just needed to escape the king's presence before he confessed what kind of idiot had joined the royal family. He'd been chosen at random to patch a problem, not carefully screened. He should put himself on a poster of what *not* to do in a bonding.

"No, thank you. I'm late for work." Sarler tried to be polite and escape before he sobbed out his story on the king's sympathetic shoulder.

"If you want to talk, come find me later," Vohne offered.

Sarler thought it over before hesitantly asking, "Wouldn't it be better to talk to your mate? I mean, as the human half of your relationship he might have better insight into my problems. I mean, if I had problems."

The king smiled, amusement dancing in his gold eyes. "I love my mate, but his idea of a relationship is running until I hunt him down. Besides, you probably know more about human and Thresl interaction than most bondmates. You just need to learn about Bleine interaction."

Sarler nodded at the wisdom of the king's statement. He would learn. He just hoped he'd learn in time.

"I might take you up on your offer later," he said. Mindful of the time, Sarler waved goodbye and rushed off to work. He knew he'd already started his day a few hours behind. Although he didn't clock in at work, he did have office hours he kept for consultation for humans who wanted to bond with a Thresl and relatives who wanted to visit their frozen loved ones.

People might be waiting for him.

A few minutes later his guess proved right.

"Hello, Earl," Sarler said with little favour. Earl had been pushing Sarler for a bonding recommendation for three months. After evaluating Earl, Sarler had determined the man didn't deserve a Thresl. He was vain, petty and had a wide mean streak. If Sarler had his way, Earl would never be allowed in the cryo-chamber to try to connect with any of the Thresl there.

"Sarl, when are you going to approve me?" he snarled.

Sarler hated it when people shortened his name, especially people who would never be his friend.

"I haven't found any Thresls I think would bond well with you," Sarler explained diplomatically. He kept hoping Earl would take the hint and move on back to whatever horrible place he originally came from. It was Sarler's belief that Earl would make a terrible bondmate, and he'd shared his views with all the other matchers so they wouldn't let him through the screening process. No one in the lab would offer Earl a Thresl, not while Sarler still breathed.

"Come on, Sarl, aren't we buddies?" A weird light filled Earl's eyes, as if he saw something no one else could see.

Creepy.

Sarler barely resisted giving in to the full body shudder threatening to tear through him.

"Earl, I'll be honest with you. I don't think you'll ever be ready for a Thresl. You don't have the right mind-set to be someone's match." Maybe honesty would work. He'd tried everything else. The emotions pouring off Earl always had a manic feel that Sarler couldn't see working well bonding with a Thresl.

A frightening look crossed Earl's face as if he'd lost control of his inner psycho and didn't plan on reining it back in anytime soon. Sarler took a large step away from Earl.

"And you do?" Earl shouted. "You were just at the right place at the right time and you bagged a prince! I have more of a right to have a Thresl than some skinny pencil pusher. How dare you hold me back from my mate!"

Earl's voice ended in a high-pitched scream of rage that had Sarler wincing at the sound. His own temper rose as he realised Earl thought he was somehow worthy because Sarler had found a bonded. Did that mean everyone on the freaking planet would now think they were worthy? It had taken several years to get humans interested in coming to the planet to mate with a Thresl after the Great Purge.

Even now, the majority of humans wanted a Thresl in cat form who would change to meet to their own specific wants and needs like a designer mate—as if they were adopting a pet—not realising that Thresls were loyal, dedicated lovers who would protect their mate until they died.

Some humans thought any match was a good match, but Sarler wanted the right mates for his cryo people. He was very protective of them. Every day he walked the length of the tubes and talked to his favourites. No way would he hand one single Thresl to the ignorant asshole before him. He gritted his teeth to hold back the words he wished to say.

Despite taking a deep breath, he lost his patience. "Thresls aren't belongings. They are sentient beings who live, love and bond with a specific human. You don't own a Thresl, you partner with one. Maybe you should try a different facility. None of the Thresls here will match with you," Sarler said in a low tone.

An odd calm wrapped around Earl like a blanket, dulling Sarler's perception. Going from raging emotions to nothing threw Sarler off. He nervously checked around, but no one else stood in the halls.

"Is that right? Not one Thresl will suit me, you think?" Earl asked.

"Yes." Sarler stood firm. No one could convince him that this idiot should mate with a Thresl. Sarler might not deserve his prince, but he'd never be intentionally cruel. He had a feeling Earl would not only be cruel but he'd enjoy it.

"Well, guess what? An opening just came up." Earl pulled a laser pistol from his jacket and shot Sarler in the chest.

Pain exploded throughout his body as Sarler tumbled to the ground. Gasping for breath, he looked up as Earl aimed, ready to shoot him again.

"What are you doing?" a voice shouted.

Sarler turned his head towards the new speaker. He couldn't form words. It hurt too much. Through the haze of pain he could make out the shape of one of the soldiers. The uniform blurred before the tears in Sarler's eyes, but he recognised the emblem on the man's shoulder as he knelt down. He felt more than saw Earl run away.

"Call a medic!" the same voice ordered. "Damn, he did a number on you, Sarler—hang in there. The prince won't forgive me if you die."

Sarler struggled to speak over the pain radiating through his body. "Tell Bleine I would've made him a good mate."

"You can tell him yourself," the soldier promised.

A loud roar echoed in the hall. Emotions raced through Sarler, feelings that didn't belong to him.

Rage. Pain. Despair.

Bleine fell to his knees beside Sarler, his gold eyes frantic with worry. Grabbing Sarler's hand centred all the emotions floating in the air and jolted through Sarler like an electric current. He would've objected, but the relief over Bleine coming for him overwhelmed all the other feelings except the pain.

"A medic is on the way. Don't you dare die on me!" Bleine shouted. His gold eyes glowed with emotion until they resembled fiery suns in Sarler's admittedly blurred vision.

"You need to go back into cryo," Sarler whispered through the searing agony in his chest. His words were slow and slurred, but he had to get his message across. "They'll find you a good mate. Ask for Dyan. He's the best."

It was important that Bleine have a good matcher. A few of them weren't as diligent in their matchups, but Sarler wouldn't take any chances with the prince. Bleine had had enough poor mates. He deserved a good one. Dyan would make sure Bleine ended up with a worthy bonded.

"You're going to live," Bleine vowed. "Where's the fucking medic? Medic!"

Bleine's swearing increased when no one magically appeared.

"We're here, your highness," a breathless voice spoke just outside Sarler's vision.

A pair of men in white scrubs moved into Sarler's view, rolling a stretcher between them. With a smooth, choreographed motion they transferred him from the ground to a firm, padded surface only slightly softer than the ground.

Sarler let out a cry of pain. Agony seared through his body, starting at his chest and radiating outward.

"Careful!" Bleine growled. "If he dies, so do you."

A look of fear crossed the face of the medic by Sarler's feet. He couldn't see the other guy but terror rolled over him from that direction, too, poking holes into Sarler's defences. Due to his injury, Sarler's usual shields were wavering. With his protections down, emotions pressed in on him from every living person in the palace, threatening to overload his brain. Sarler closed his eyes, trying to shut off all outside stimuli. He struggled, heart pounding, to raise his shields again. He couldn't. Fear, anxiety and Bleine's despair swamped him. Unable to handle the pressure, he succumbed as everything went white.

"Sarler!" Bleine's frantic shout echoed in his ears before he lost consciousness.

"He'll be fine, your highness," the medic said once again.

Bleine nodded even if he didn't believe the man. How could Sarler be fine? He had an open wound in his chest and brutal seizures were making his eyes roll back into his head. Bleine touched his mate hoping skin contact would soothe him. It seemed to end the convulsions at least.

"Come on, honey, you can get through this. We'll get you all healed up and better in no time," he promised in a low tone.

The link between them, tenuous before, stretched even thinner. He could almost see the string reaching its breaking point, but Bleine refused to give up. They still had issues to work through, problems he couldn't fix on his own.

"Hold on, mate," Bleine whispered as he raced alongside the stretcher back to the medic wing of the castle. He didn't want to disturb their concentration by talking too loudly. Not when his entire life depended on Sarler's survival. He needed the empath to open his eyes and glare at him. Even a look of total disdain would make everything better. Anything. Any sign of his mate reviving would lift the weight off Bleine's chest. Regret knifed through his chest as he remembered how they had separated earlier. If they'd stayed in bed to work things out, Sarler wouldn't have been there to face the psychopath who had shot him.

Sarler could die and Bleine would never be able to tell him how much he needed him. If he lost Sarler, he'd wander into the forest to die so his brother wouldn't try to save him again. Three bondmates was his limit. His Thresl DNA had been stretched as far as possible to accommodate his human half. Now he needed to move on, either to properly bond with Sarler or to let him go and end his own existence.

He'd done his duty to his people. Vohne and Kres were strong enough to hold the kingdom together. They were probably strong enough to take care of a couple of planets between them and have the energy to quell any uprising that dared to thwart their power. Bleine smiled as he thought of the love between the royal duo. If only he could find the same success in his own match.

As the medics pushed Sarler through the double doors, Bleine held back. He couldn't watch them stitch up his mate. His stomach churned uneasily. If he never saw Sarler bleeding on the floor again it would be too soon.

He'd watched one mate die already. The memory of his first bonded — bright, vibrant Klia, who had died in his arms from a stomach wound — struck him hard. He couldn't lose another.

He just couldn't.

Taking a deep breath, he tried to gather his inner calm. He needed to stay strong for his mate. If Sarler woke and experienced Bleine's despair, it could cause psychological damage or make him try to find Bleine and help him. Empaths tended to have fewer instincts for self-preservation than other specialities.

A large hand gripped his shoulder. Bleine turned to meet his brother's eyes. Kres stood beside Vohne, his expression solemn.

"We heard," Vohne said. He pulled Bleine into a tight hug that threatened to crack his bones, before releasing him. "There's an alert out to find Earl. He escaped the palace when everyone was focused on Sarler. It will be harder to find him in the city, but with enough eyes looking out for him, we should get him into custody soon."

Bleine growled in frustration. His anger spiked and burned with the heat of a spaceship rocket. He longed for his claws again so he could tear apart the man responsible for harming his mate. For a second his fingertips tingled, distracting him.

"We'll catch him, Bleine. If he's in the city, he'll be hunted down and brought to justice," Vohne promised.

Bleine didn't care about justice. He wanted death.

He shook his head to try to clear the dark spots from his mind. This wasn't him. He'd used diplomacy and persuasion his entire career. Why now did he wish such destruction?

"You okay, Bleine?" Kres asked.

"I think so." Bleine didn't mention his rage. How could he explain how uncomfortable his skin had suddenly become around him? Was he changing for Sarler? Did something in his gentle empath's future need Bleine to be more warrior than peacemaker? Neither humans nor Thresl kind had ever properly deciphered the way of the Thresl change, and now, with his mate's life in danger, Bleine had little interest in deciphering the puzzles of his DNA.

"Here's the medic," Vohne murmured.

Bleine's head snapped up and he forced his attention to the present. No use worrying, he would eventually become what Sarler needed through little shifts in his personality and build. Unfortunately, since Sarler wasn't Bleine's original mate he wouldn't be able to form a more pleasing shape. He couldn't become the woman of Sarler's preference. He brushed aside his negative thoughts. Now wasn't about him. It was about his mate.

The human medic had pretty salt and pepper hair and piercing blue eyes filled with compassion. Bleine knew the man had been working for them for three years since his Thresl mate had died in a rare space shuttle accident. His name was Richard or Ronaan or something like that.

"Your majesties." The medic gave a half bow to the trio before turning his attention to Bleine. "Your mate Sarler is going to be fine. We've sealed his wound. Some internal tenderness will continue for a few weeks, but after a transfusion and some mild painkillers, he'll be good to take home tomorrow."

Relief swept through Bleine. He hadn't realised how tightly he'd been clenching his muscles until he relaxed them all.

"I need to see him." The urge to set eyes on his mate clawed at him with a compulsion that wouldn't be denied.

The medic nodded. "Right this way."

Bleine followed the man down the hall until he reached Sarler's room. Peeking through the doorway his breath caught in his throat at the sight of his bonded looking so pale. Careful not to wake Sarler, Bleine approached the bed silently. He couldn't resist wrapping his fingers around Sarler's left hand, mindful of the tubes attached to hydrate and medicate his body.

"I'm so sorry I didn't protect you," he whispered. What kind of Thresl couldn't protect the ones he loved? That was his biggest failure and apparently one he continued to make. He would insist on guards for Sarler until they apprehended Earl. He couldn't risk losing his bonded. They'd been lucky this time that someone had intervened. If the person who'd found Sarler hadn't interrupted, Earl could've ended his life.

Bleine kissed Sarler's forehead, relishing the brush of silky skin beneath his lips.

Sarler's eyes fluttered open. His first glimpse of Bleine brought a smile to his face.

"I had a dream you were beside me," he whispered as if not wanting to break the peacefulness of the moment.

"What was I doing?" Bleine asked, curious about Sarler's inner thoughts. Did he have pleasant dreams or did he stress about his mating with a useless Thresl who couldn't keep him safe? Bleine bit his lip to hold back words better left unsaid.

"You were lying in bed and holding me close." As Sarler smiled at the memory, his expression—eyes soft from sleep and drugs—went directly to Bleine's libido. He bet that was how Sarler looked in the morning when his mate didn't foolishly get into a fight with him.

"We can make that a reality soon," Bleine promised. "They're going to let you go home to heal tomorrow. You'll be coming to stay with me."

Where he belonged.

Bleine didn't leave any room for questions and from the gentle smile he received, Sarler didn't mind.

"Okay," Sarler agreed. "Am I going to be all right?"

Bleine nodded. Unable to resist, he brushed the hair away from Sarler's face. "Yeah, the medic says you'll be sore for a while, but there will be no permanent damage. They got to you in time."

Tears prickled at Bleine's eyes, but he blinked them back, hoping Sarler didn't see the weakness in his mate. He needed to be strong for his other half.

"Good. I'd hate for you to have a damaged mate," Sarler said. "You deserve the best."

"The best for me is you. I'm sorry about before. About the fight." Bleine stumbled over his words, wishing once again he could be as smooth with his life partner as he could with planetary rulers. Something about Sarler always had him stumbling over his own tongue.

Sarler tightened his fingers around Bleine's hand. "When I was shot, all I could think about was not leaving you alone. I wanted you to find a proper mate. One who doesn't have hang-ups about having a male mate because of his upbringing. A true partner who could give you everything you are looking for. Now that I made it, I selfishly want to keep you all to myself."

The nervous look on Sarler's face reassured Bleine more than any flowery words ever could.

"We'll work things out," Bleine promised.

A warm smile crossed Sarler's lips and his eyes lit up with joy. "Yes, we will."

It wasn't unheard of for mates to be incompatible, but it was extremely rare. Bleine wanted Sarler to know he wouldn't trap them in this relationship. Sarler always had a choice. "I can have Vohne dissolve our bond if you truly wish to be alone," he offered.

"That would kill you!" Sarler protested. "I know enough about Thresls to know you wouldn't survive that kind of separation. I refuse to let you do that. It might take me a little while to get used to a male mate, but I'm attracted to you."

Bleine smiled as relief rushed through him. If they weren't sexually compatible, things would've been much harder to work out. The fact Sarler wanted him calmed his beast. His inner cat yearned for its mate's affection.

"Hey"—Sarler squeezed his grip on Bleine's arm— "we will work things out, I promise. We just had a rockier start than most."

Bleine knew Sarler must be experiencing his anxiety. He took a long, slow breath to try to bring down his tension level. Sarler had enough pain without Bleine adding to his stress.

Bleine nodded. He'd see how things went. If life became unbearable he could probably convince Vohne to break the bond.

Maybe.

His brother became stubborn sometimes.

"I'm going to let you take a nap now. I'll come back and get you before you know it," Bleine promised.

He couldn't sit there beside Sarler. He'd end up saying something stupid and needy. Now that he knew Sarler was out of danger, he was ready to get back to work and try to bury himself in his research.

Bleine was trying to find the lost writings of the ancient Thresls. So far all he could find were a few footnotes in other manuscripts about the upcoming battle for the heart of the Thresls. He'd originally thought the author had been referring to the Great Purge, but further research seemed to suggest otherwise. He wished he could find the earlier writings by the seers, but they had vanished during their father's lifetime.

Kissing Sarler's forehead, Bleine promised to come see him later.

Chapter Three

A nurse woke him in the middle of the night with a shot for the pain. Sarler hadn't been aware he'd been in pain until she had woken him up. He resisted the urge to snarl at her. After all, even half asleep he knew it was a bad idea to anger the person in charge of giving him medication.

Of course, if he'd been truly bonded with Bleine he'd have had enhanced healing and wouldn't have needed so much medication. Stupid him. Hopefully the palace gossipmongers weren't already nattering on about their poor mating.

After he recovered, Sarler would make sure to let the prince know how much he appreciated Bleine's patience. The prince deserved a better mate than a sexually repressed empath, but Sarler would make sure he made everything up to Bleine in the future. The attack had at least one good thing come from it. His bonded was willing to talk to him now.

"You don't have to bond with him, you know," the nurse interrupted Sarler's thoughts.

"What?" Surely he had misunderstood her.

She gave him a sly smile. "The prince. You don't have to bond with him. It isn't too late to transfer him to another, maybe a woman who can give him children. You're a matcher. I'm sure you could find him a replacement if the thought of having a male mate is too much for you."

He didn't like her insinuation. Give Bleine to someone else indeed! Agitation coursed through Sarler at the nurse's words. "He's mine!" he snapped. How dare she consider anyone else touching his prince!

Stunned at his strong reaction, Sarler raised a hand to cover his mouth in shock. He'd never yelled at anyone in his life.

"I see." An amused glint lit the nurse's eyes. "I'm glad you're loyal. The prince deserves to finally have a proper mate."

"Were you testing me?" Sarler asked. Why would she pry into his relationship with the prince? Was she looking for holes in their relationship? Sarler jumped from mostly sleepy to fully awake as he examined the nurse.

"Those of us protecting the Thresls have to protect them against the ones who wish them harm," she said mysteriously. "I've watched over the Thresls since my mother gave me the job as a child. If you had planned to harm him, I would've killed you and tried to quickly find a replacement. Word around the palace is there's some doubt as to your compatibility. We can't have the prince torn away from his duty to coddle an uncertain mate. The prince needs someone he can count on."

Fear raced through Sarler. It only increased when she leaned closer, her eyes lit with an almost fanatical light. The drugs had dulled Sarler's empathic abilities.

He couldn't sense her emotions. He was essentially blind to what she was feeling. For the first time he realised how regular people felt. It was as if he were missing a limb.

It didn't calm him any when she glanced around to make sure no one was near. Just as he was contemplating screaming for the guards, the nurse pulled a necklace from beneath her top. On a thin gold chain dangled a gold claw pendant. "We are the Threslan, children of Thresls and their human mates who are born as human. We live to protect our bonded kin, both human and Thresl. Our numbers were too few during the Great Purge so we were unable to save all our brethren, but we are stronger now and know how to keep an eye out for those who threaten our people."

Sarler had heard of the Threslan before. Most of the time Thresl blood overpowered human genes, and even those with a minor amount of Thresl DNA were born in cat form. However, a small minority were born in their human shape like regular babies, never experienced transition and tended to only have minor Thresl traits. In other cultures they would be cast aside as mutants, but the Thresls cherished all children.

"Who are you?" He didn't know if he trusted this redheaded woman. Examining her more closely, he saw her eyes were green with stripes of gold. She definitely had Thresl blood, but he didn't trust easily, especially with drugs in his system dulling his usual perception.

"I'm Dina," she introduced herself.

"Sarler."

"I know you. Everyone knows you. It's hard to mate with a prince and not become instantly famous."

Sarler wasn't sure how he felt about that. He'd always been a private person, almost aggressively introverted. Dina did have a point, though. He was foolish to have thought he could stay out of the limelight for long. To be the other half of a Thresl prince was an intimidating thing, even without including the male lover issue.

Dina patted Sarler's leg. "Get some rest and take this." She gave him a small, square, plastic black box on a key chain.

"It's an alert necklace. If you ever get into a situation where you think your life is in danger, smash this box and one of us will come save you."

"Thanks." He accepted the alarm even as he wondered how she could possibly help. Dina didn't look like she could survive a hard breeze, much less come to his rescue.

"I'm tougher than I look." She gave him a knowing smile as if she could read his mind, patted his leg then walked out of the room.

Sarler set the keychain on his side table.

He remembered those good days when he'd only had to worry if the person frozen in cryo suffered or not. Bleine had always drawn Sarler's attention. The fact that he'd stepped briefly away to check on another person when Bleine's cryo chamber had been smashed didn't make him feel any better about his mate's condition when they'd bonded. Or the fact he'd connected so strongly with Bleine that he'd been incapacitated by convulsions on the floor when the psycho woman had smashed Bleine's cryo tank.

If they had bonded under normal conditions Sarler would've been proud to have been chosen as a Thresl mate, even a male one. However, with Bleine forced to accept him, Sarler didn't feel he had the same rights as a proper bondmate chosen with care.

Sarler closed his eyes, ready for another nap. He wanted to be alert when Bleine came for him in the morning. The next thing he knew he was waking to the sound of someone talking.

"Sarler...wake up, honey, it's time to go home." Bleine's deep voice slithered into Sarler's dreams. The prince's warm energy wrapped him in a happy glow. Even half asleep he derived comfort from Bleine's presence. His battered body might ache and twist in pain, but his soul basked in sound of Bleine's rich baritone. The drugs must've worn off during his sleep because Bleine's worry telegraphed clearly into Sarler's head.

When Sarler didn't immediately open his eyes, Bleine's tone turned harder and his concern turned more frantic.

"Don't make me try to find another bondmate. Third time is supposed to be lucky. I won't survive a fourth. Besides, Kres said he'd kill me if I made Vohne suffer that way again," Bleine said.

The prince sounded more amused than concerned about potential murder by his brother-in-law. From what he'd heard of Kres, Bleine might be taking the threat too lightly. The king-mate was notoriously protective of his Thresl.

Sarler wanted to see Bleine's expression. The handsome prince rarely had smiles for him. Anxiety always filled Bleine's eyes whenever he saw Sarler. He'd done that to the sweet prince—had undermined the confident man who'd worked so hard to hold his people together in his brother's absence. He'd hurt him. Everyone he'd talked to had congratulated Sarler on his bonding with envy in their eyes and lies conveying happiness on their lips. Sarler could read their disdain for him to have been chosen above all others. They each thought they'd make a better choice than him in Bleine's bed.

He still didn't know why the king-mate had chosen Sarler of all the people in the room to bond with the prince when Bleine's chamber had shattered. But he did know that he'd never gather enough guts to question Kreslan personally. The king-mate had a feral intensity about him stronger than any Thresl Sarler had ever met. Frankly, he frightened Sarler a little. He'd find it too overwhelming to question Kres' actions no matter what they might be.

"Sarler. Honey. Wake up." Bleine's impatience pricked at him like tiny needles, urging him to open his eyes and face the day.

"I'm awake. Stop poking at me," Sarler grumbled.

"Trust me, mate. If I were poking you we'd both be having a whole lot more fun." Bleine's dry tone had Sarler's eyes snapping open.

"Very funny," he said, meeting Bleine's amused gaze.

Gold eyes, like trapped sunshine, glowed at him. He wondered if anyone had ever been burned by a Thresl's stare. The man's eyes were hot and intense as if his gaze could scorch Sarler in all the right ways.

Despite the gentle manner Bleine used with him, Sarler could feel licks of desire lapping at him like fiery tongues.

"Stop that!" Sarler complained. "I don't want to leave the ward with an erection."

Bleine's smile, slow and sweet, made his attraction all the more dangerous. How could he stay upset with a man who smiled with the open joy of a birthday surprise? He was glad Bleine hoarded his smiles because Sarler greedily didn't want him to share them with just anyone. Bleine exuded happiness like the sun gave off heat, sunning Sarler's soul with warmth.

"I could always take care of your…ummm…problem," Bleine purred, his deep voice going even deeper until Sarler could feel it in his loins.

"That's not helping," Sarler growled in frustration. The image in his head of Bleine lapping and sucking at his erection only made him harder.

"I am an excellent helper," Bleine argued his case.

"Can I get out of here now?" Sarler asked, unwilling to hear all the details of how Bleine could help him out. He knew without a doubt that Bleine would be more than happy to share his ideas until Sarler came all over the bedding.

"I brought you some clothes."

Sarler hadn't noticed the brown satchel in Bleine's hands before. The thought of the prince going to his tiny, messy quarters to get his things made him blush. "I haven't picked up my place in a while," he admitted, blushing.

Bleine smiled. "I liked it. It smelt like you."

Wow, that definitely didn't help his morning wood. Only a Thresl would be charmed with the stench of his mate's clothes tossed about. Shaking his head, Sarler slid out of bed and accepted the bag Bleine held out. Surprisingly the prince had picked out Sarler's favourite outfit of blue denim and a soft red shirt that kept him warm no matter how cool the room. He wore it often to his job when he worked in the cryo room.

At his enquiring look, Bleine shrugged. "They smelt like you the most."

That made sense. He determinedly didn't look up at Bleine while he dressed despite the waves of desire pouring off the Thresl. He didn't want to see the need in Bleine's eyes—not while he was standing half-dressed in a hospital room and couldn't do anything about it. At the last minute he slid the black box into his pocket.

He wanted to wait and explore their bond when they were alone in Bleine's room. A quick glance in the bag revealed toiletries were in there along with his clothing.

"Aren't you taking me home?" He didn't really want to go home. He just wanted Bleine to confirm he was going back to his suite. He hoped to eventually take all his things over to Bleine's place. They needed to be together to build their bond and explore who they were as a couple. Sarler wanted to be Bleine's friend as well as his mate. He only hoped it was possible after his mistakes of before.

He darted a quick glance at Bleine in time to see the prince nod his head. "I'm taking you to my suite while you heal. We should be together."

"All right," Sarler agreed. He tried to keep his smile to controllable levels. After all, he was getting what he wanted and, even better, it was Bleine's idea.

"I'd like you to move in with me permanently," Bleine said in a quiet voice.

"I'd like that too," Sarler replied. "I know we started out shaky and I'm sorry if you thought I pitied you. I didn't. I'm just...awkward." He didn't know how else to put it. He had minimal social skills and the ones he had were rough. He definitely wasn't attached to his small apartment. He'd only lived there a few weeks and hadn't even personalised it yet. It certainly didn't feel like home, not like Bleine's suite did. Bleine had probably lived in his lodgings for hundreds of years and had had plenty of time to make them his own.

Bleine nodded, happiness pouring off him again. From his studies, Sarler knew Thresls loved to provide for their mates. By allowing Bleine to procure him a place to live, Sarler had soothed Bleine's beast's nature.

Thresl mating was a tricky thing and Sarler was still going through all the documentation he could find on mating rituals. As much as he counselled the Thresls at the cryo lab, discussing a Thresl bond and living with one turned out to be worlds apart. He had a lot more sympathy for those bonded with a difficult match.

With Bleine, at least he had an honestly great guy, even for a royal. No one in the palace could say Bleine didn't do his best for his people. The prince had worked himself to the bone to save the Thresls and hold his brother's position of power. Many would've taken the kingdom as their own, but Bleine's faith that his brother would return had never wavered.

Sarler wondered what it was like to have that much belief in another person. From stories he'd overheard, Bleine had never faltered, his conviction steadfast over the long decades. If Sarler could get even half of that devotion pointed towards him, he'd live a happy life.

They just had to get over the hurdle of one of them not being a woman.

Memories of some of his recent dreams had Sarler blushing. He definitely didn't have any problem with Bleine being male in those.

Sarler moved slowly to put on his shoes, grateful when Bleine knelt down and helped him. The shards of pain in his chest made him ask, "Are you sure I'm going to be fine?"

Sarler knew Bleine wouldn't lie. Even without his empathic abilities.

"You'll be fine," Bleine assured him. "Give it a few months and you'll be all completely healed. Of course, if we were properly bonded you would heal quicker."

The reproof in Bleine's voice projected his disappointment.

Sarler decided to lay it all out on the table. As he told the people he counselled, you couldn't work through issues if you swept them under the rug. Taking a deep breath, he revealed his greatest fear.

"I didn't think you'd want to bond with me. You've always had women in the past." Beautiful women. Sarler had seen pictures of the previous princesses. Even though Bleine's last mate Jallryne had turned out to be a power hungry psychopath, she'd still been lovely.

"What about you?" Bleine countered, pinning Sarler in place with his vibrant gold eyes. "I was told you preferred the female sex also."

Sarler sighed. Now was the time for confession. There could only be truth between them if they wanted to make their relationship work. "I don't know what I prefer. I've always dated women in the past because anything else wasn't acceptable on my home world. I've never been intimate with anyone before."

Bleine's mouth dropped open. "You've never had sex?" The prince's astonishment drifted through Sarler like a spring cloud.

"I'm an empath," Sarler reminded him.

"I know, but you're not a eunuch," Bleine exclaimed. Shock showed on his face, as if he'd discovered a bizarre creature had wandered into his palace and he didn't know what to do with such a strange beast.

Sarler sighed. "I can feel everything my lover feels. If she's uncomfortable or nervous, it doubles my anxiety. It's hard to have sex with someone when you know what they feel about your every move."

"What about when we slept together?" Bleine asked. "Did you feel anxious?"

"No," Sarler said in surprise as he reflected on their night in bed. Memories of warmth, affection and complete contentment filled him. "I enjoyed sleeping with you."

"Good. I plan to hold you every night in the future. If you're willing." Bleine's anxiety trickled over to him and he realised the prince wasn't as confident as he projected. Pleased, Sarler smiled. At least they were both in the same predicament over their relationship. Not that Bleine could abandon him or anything, but bonding didn't necessarily have to be a happy thing. He'd met a few Thresls who'd had bonding remorse. It didn't happen often but when it did, it was ugly.

"I'm willing. I want this to work." How many times could he say that? They both were spending so much time reassuring the other that they weren't really listening.

Bleine stroked a finger down Sarler's cheek, leaving a searing path of need behind. "I know I'm not what or who you would've chosen for a partner, but I'm here and willing to give you as much time as you need. We have centuries to spend together. We don't have to figure it all out right away."

"Thanks." Tension eased out of him. The fact that Bleine knew he needed time and was willing to give it to him eased the worry grinding away in his stomach.

Bleine patted Sarler's arm. "Come on, they've done what they can for you. Let's get you home so you can get some rest. You probably need sleep and food more than anything else right now."

Sarler smiled. "I could eat."

He could also enjoy snuggling next to Bleine. He liked the idea of having a home to return to with a gorgeous prince waiting for him at the end of the day. Of course, Bleine might not appreciate living with a slob. Sarler made a mental note to focus on becoming tidier.

The comfort flowing from the prince seeped into Sarler's brain, more soothing than a gallon of sedatives.

"Ready?"

Sarler nodded then smiled when Bleine wrapped an arm around his waist to help him out of bed. Bleine's sudden focused attention almost made him want to thank Earl for the injury. Straightening too quickly caused a spike of pain to rip through him.

Maybe not.

"We'll walk slowly," Bleine promised. "Do you want me to get you a floater?"

Another twinge had Sarler nodding. He couldn't walk all that way. "Sorry."

"Why?" Bleine asked, looking genuinely puzzled. "You were shot. There's nothing wrong with asking for help."

"Thanks," Sarler said as Bleine vanished to go get him a floating chair.

Despite his words, he doubted the prince asked for help very often. Bleine probably had self-sufficiency down to an art form. Sarler wondered what he could do to make things easier for the prince. What part could he play in the prince's life outside of the bedroom? He'd eventually have to learn to move in political circles and be able to talk to people in power. He didn't have any problems talking to Bleine or even the king. They were good rulers who cared about their people. Throwing himself into the shark pit of the court was a different matter.

"What are you worrying about?" Bleine asked as he entered the room with the floater. Floaters were like small sleighs made to adjust for people who needed to get around but couldn't walk. The old, the infirm and the newly injured often used them throughout the palace.

Sarler shook his head. "Nothing. I'm fine."

Bleine gave him a knowing look but didn't insist Sarler shared what he was thinking. He'd never been so glad of anything in his life. He wasn't quite ready to expose all his insecurities at once. Better to let the prince discover them a little at a time. No one wanted to learn their mate was a basket-case right away.

Careful of his injury, Sarler slid onto the chair. It dipped a second before rising to accommodate Sarler's weight. The padded chair proved to be oddly comfortable as whatever the material it was made from inflated to cradle him.

"Easy now." Bleine pushed Sarler back when he leaned too far forward.

"Sorry. I've never ridden in one of these before," Sarler explained.

"You haven't done a lot of things, honey," Bleine said.

"True." Sarler wasn't about to object to Bleine's gentle teasing when the prince appeared to be looking forward to educating him.

Sarler floated down the hall using the hand controls to follow Bleine. Without the prince to guide him, he doubted he'd have found his way. He didn't have the best sense of direction.

Bleine stopped outside the door of his suite. Sarler recognised the familiar double doors and the soldiers standing outside. They'd let him in the night before.

"Gentlemen, this is my mate Sarler. Sarler, these are Friln and Nelrin. They usually guard my brother, but I've asked them to give you special protection until Earl is found."

Sarler frowned. "I'm a soldier, you know. I can protect myself. I just wasn't expecting an attack." He might not be a military genius, but he'd been trained in basic hand-to-hand combat and weapon usage. Pointing and shooting a man didn't take a genius level IQ—he just had to avoid being shot first.

"I know you can. They are here for my peace of mind," Bleine said in a soothing tone that fooled no one.

Bleine's anxiety slammed into Sarler like a sledgehammer. He knew without asking that the prince wouldn't be able to rest if Sarler didn't have at least this pair of guards watching over him. Biting back the scathing retort begging to trip off his tongue, Sarler nodded his acceptance. "Thank you," he said to the guards.

Bleine smiled at the pair before leading Sarler inside.

"Let's get you comfortable in bed. I'll feed you and then let you get some rest," Bleine said.

"I bet you say that to all the guys," Sarler teased.

"I assure you I've never said that to another man before," Bleine replied.

Sarler smiled in relief. "I keep forgetting this is as new for you as it is for me."

That shouldn't have made him feel as good as it did, but he liked the idea they were experiencing something new together. Despite Bleine's long life, there were still things he hadn't done before. Sarler liked being Bleine's first in at least one way. With a much older mate, Sarler knew Bleine had done tons of things he'd never even contemplated. That he hadn't been intimate with a man before made their relationship special in its own way.

"You can feel my emotions. You know I want you here," Bleine insisted.

Sarler mentally reached out to scan Bleine's mind. Worry, a touch of anxiety and the warm glow of affection wrapped around Sarler like sunshine.

"I know." Sarler gripped Bleine's shoulder in a reassuring hold. "I can feel your bond with me. We can do this together."

He almost choked on the words, but he knew they were the right ones to say. He wouldn't leave Bleine worrying that Sarler was going to try to trick him or leave him. Bleine had enough stress without his mate playing games.

Relief rushed from Bleine, so thick it almost choked Sarler. "Easy, mate," Sarler said through the fog of emotions. His shields that he'd built back up after the surgery began to weaken beneath Bleine's strong feelings. Over time Sarler knew he'd no longer have walls keeping Bleine out. They would co-exist as two harmonious parts of one person. For now—while still recovering—he planned to take it slow. He wondered if Bleine would agree.

"Let's get you healed first then we can work on us," Bleine said as if reading Sarler's mind.

Sarler laughed then winced at the motion. "You sound like a counsellor. Are you trying to take my job?"

"I'm nervous," Bleine admitted.

"Stressing won't help matters," Sarler said. "We're both interested in our bond. We have a lifetime to work out the kinks."

Bleine cupped Sarler's face between his palms. "Nothing is more important to me than us. Now get into bed, I'll order you some food then I want you to get some sleep. I have boring meetings to attend and a monarchy to stabilise."

"Ahh, the glamorous life of a prince," Sarler said.

"Yep. I can barely stand under all the glitter and gold." Bleine kissed Sarler, a hot, hard embrace that left both of them panting.

Sarler's heart pounded against his chest. "I-I'm going to get into bed and rest."

"The video feed is behind that wall and you'll find the remote in the side table."

"I'll be fine." Sarler waved Bleine away.

Bleine kissed Sarler. When they finally parted, Sarler's body ached with need and his mouth tingled from the press of their lips.

Sarler licked his lips trying to capture the sensation again. Kissing Bleine went to his head more than the most potent wine.

"You taste amazing." A purr rolled up from Bleine's throat.

Sarler's cock hardened even further as if conditioned to that sound. If Bleine made that noise while fucking him, Sarler knew he wouldn't last long. The thought of having sex with Bleine excited him. He needed Bleine's big body pinning him to the bed and the prince's soft lips brushing across his skin. The contrast of firm and gentle that only the prince could give him.

Damn.

"I'll see you later. Take it easy." Bleine kissed Sarler on the top of the head as if he knew a trap waited for him with Sarler's lips.

Sarler tried not to pout as he grabbed the remote to find something to watch.

Chapter Four

Bleine headed for his brother's office, secure in the knowledge that his mate was well watched over. He found Vohne at his desk and Vohne's mate Kreslan lounging on the couch watching him.

"Hello, brother," Vohne greeted him. "How's Sarler?"

"He's healing. It will take a while, but the medics are anticipating a full recovery."

"Did you tuck him at your place?" Vohne's inquiring expression had Bleine revealing more. His brother always knew how to get Bleine to confess everything with little effort.

"I'm optimistic about our relationship now. He says he's willing to give us a try." Bleine couldn't stop the smile stretching his lips. Just saying the words gave him a warm glow. If Sarler hadn't been injured, Bleine would've wanted to test that new resolve this morning. Instead he'd left his sexy man all alone in his bed.

"Good. I've got some news for you. I received a report that Earl was spotted just outside the city by the old ruins. I think he's trying to hide out until this all blows over and maybe try to either escape off planet or attack again. He doesn't strike me as the type to give up, so I'm guessing he's going to try to get at Sarler. I think we need to hunt him down and arrest him. We need to send a message that it's not all right to attack any member of the royal family."

The grim set of Vohne's mouth told Bleine his brother had more than one reason for his statement, but a glance over at Kres, who shook his head warningly, had Bleine keeping silent.

As Vohne rifled around in his desk looking for something, Bleine examined his brother. It always jolted him, the little differences that took place during each transformation. It had taken Bleine a few days to get used to his brother's new name. Kres, however, was the real surprise. The king-mate had always been a gentler soul before. This new Kres with his weapon proficiency and pragmatic approach to things threw him a bit. In previous lives, Kres had been a painter, or a poet. Once he'd become a horse trainer. Never had he returned as a soldier before.

This version of his brother-in-law had dangerous edges Bleine doubted any amount of time would ever smooth away. Kres gave him a friendly wave from where he lay on the couch but continued to casually twirl a knife in his hand.

"Any new information on your overthrow?" Bleine asked cheerfully. He had a difficult time brooding when his mate lay tucked into his bed.

Vohne shook his head at Bleine's levity. "I'm not any closer to figuring out who helped keep me from connecting with Kres for the last century."

"Besides the psycho who woke you from cryo," Kres tossed in.

Bleine sat in the chair across from Vohne's desk. "Who are our suspects?"

"We don't really have any...or rather, we have too many. Most of the people who participated in the Great Purge are candidates, those who resent being bound to humans, humans who resent being bound to Thresls... Many people might want the monarchy, to either take the spot themselves or to establish a new leadership," Vohne said, frustration evident on his face.

"What are we going to do? If you want to fight to keep the monarchy, the majority of people are on your side." Bleine couldn't even imagine his brother's despair over returning to a world that had moved on in his absence. A world that didn't welcome its king as joyfully as it had in the past.

"To tell you the truth, I don't care about being king," Vohne confessed. "I've been the ruler for centuries. If others want to try a hand at the job, I'm more than willing to let them, as long as they have the best interests of the Thresl in mind."

"How would we know, though?" Bleine asked. "When pressure came to do the right thing, most of them failed us. They either hid with their mates or they joined the dissenters. Few stayed and fought beside me."

Bleine still had nightmares of the carnage around him, of the dead humans collapsing and bringing on the death of their Thresls. Bleine had rushed from couple to couple, hoping to save people in time. Some he'd been able to give shots to and put in cryo before they had a complete breakdown, but they'd lost so many...thousands they'd been unable to save.

Vohne leaned his head against the back of his chair. "I just want to spend time with my mate."

Exhaustion was evident in Vohne's voice even as he smiled over at Kres. The affection in his eyes when he watched his mate gave Bleine hope for his own relationship. Vohne had ever been a difficult man. A man of strong passions, stubborn, short-tempered and obsessively protective of his mate. Kres' previous incarnations had balanced Vohne with a softer, gentler demeanour. Now it appeared they'd switched places and Vohne was the less aggressive half of the royal pair.

Bleine kind of liked this new version.

If they were truly in their final resurrection, there would be another war coming. The prophecy clearly stated they were the harbinger of the final battle for the future of Thresl kind.

"I need to do more research," Bleine said. He'd always been the scholarly one of the family. Assassins had killed their parents when they were young, leaving the two brothers to fend for themselves. Over time they'd established a rhythm between them. Bleine studied law and history, and Vohne handled military strategy and politics.

"Would you like to be king?" Kres asked him, his tone calm and easy.

Bleine relaxed. His brother-in-law wasn't accusing him of being power-hungry—Kres was only being curious.

"Not particularly. I was king in all but name for a hundred years. I was happy to hand it back over to Vohne."

"Too bad," Vohne mused. "At least we know you'd have the planet's best interests at heart."

"What about the other families? There's an entire royal hierarchy, isn't there? I know I met a bunch of them when I arrived." Kres lifted an eyebrow at his mate.

Bleine laughed. Kres' disdain for royalty was only muted for Vohne and Bleine. He held the rest of the ruling class in more than a little dislike. At least one of them, probably more, had plotted to prevent Vohne's return home. Kres tended to blame the entire group for not stepping in and doing something to protect their king. From what Bleine could tell, Kres didn't have a forgiving soul when it came to people messing with his mate.

Now they still had to plan a wedding ceremony and figure out how to thwart their enemies.

"We should plan your wedding. We've put it off long enough with all the other problems that arose," Bleine announced.

"Ow...fuck." Kres held up his bleeding finger. "You could warn a guy."

Vohne laughed. He pulled a bandage out of his drawer and handed it to Kres.

"Kres, could you do me a favour and drop in on Sarler?" Bleine asked. "He's recovering in my suite."

"Sure." Kres wrapped his finger and gave it an annoyed scowl as if the injury was a personal affront.

"Could you do it now?" Vohne prompted.

"Darling, if you want to talk to your brother alone you only had to ask. Subtle you are not." Kres stood up and walked over to kiss Vohne's forehead. Shaking his head, Kres left the room.

"Thanks, Kres!" Bleine yelled after him.

Vohne eyed Bleine with interest. "Why do you want Kres to check on your man?"

"I figure if Sarler has at least one friend he'll be happier," Bleine replied.

"How do you know he doesn't have friends? Not to mention, are you certain Kres is the best choice? I adore my mate but he can be…abrasive," Vohne said even as his eyes flickered back to the door as if he could catch one more glimpse of his beloved.

"Sarler moved here only a few months ago. He didn't have time to meet very many people," Bleine explained.

"And now with his quick bonding with you and the attack, his chances for friendship haven't improved much," Vohne concluded. "Poor guy. Well, Kres will make him feel safe at least, and they have something in common—neither of them wanted to mate with a Thresl."

Bleine gave a bitter laugh. "At least yours is fated. I seem to just stumble along and bond with the wrong people."

Vohne shook his head. "I have a good feeling about this one. Sarler is a good guy. I think it'll work out in the end."

"First we need to catch Earl. He can't be allowed to run free. I'm going to head out there and see if I can track him down. Maybe if Sarler feels more secure, he'll bond with me easier." Bleine didn't need to convey to his brother how badly he wanted this to work. Vohne understood the need to please a mate.

"Take some guards with you. I don't know how dangerous the old ruins might be. Have you explored them recently?" Vohne asked.

Bleine had to think it over. Strangely enough, despite enjoying archaeology, he'd never given the ruins much thought, except as a place to clear out the thieves and vagrants that tended to live in their shadows. The remains were mostly underground, but some of the outer walls still stood.

"Not really. Which is strange when you think about it. I mean, it's been there for centuries and even as children we didn't go explore."

The more he thought about it, the stranger it was, as if they'd overlooked a piece of their heritage for no better reason than they hadn't thought about it.

"You know the locals think it's haunted," Vohne reminded him. "Maybe you're just afraid of the ghost." Vohne made spooky noises.

Bleine rolled his eyes. "Next you're going to dare me to explore the treacherous ruins where I'll probably break an ankle and have to be laid up in bed myself, if I don't break my neck. And what about you, big, bad king? Why haven't you explored?"

Vohne shrugged. "Time. It went down to the bottom of my list. Like you said, for some reason I'd never thought of it before."

"Do you think it's spelled?" For two curious Thresls to pretty much avoid a place that might have relics of their past was unheard of, and now that Bleine was thinking about it, he was certain there had to be another reason they had overlooked an entire burned down palace.

"I'm almost sure of it now. Which makes me wonder—if Earl is hiding there perhaps the spell is starting to fade. I want you to check out both the possible presence of Sarler's attacker, and the palace itself if you get the chance. Don't go anywhere you might get hurt. Whether it's spelled or not, it's still a crumbling structure."

Bleine nodded. "I'll be careful."

"Good and take some guards with you. That way you can trap Earl between you. I know you want to take revenge for your mate, but be practical."

"I will." Bleine's first urge was to hunt down Earl and rip out his heart, but Vohne had a good point. If the man got away because Bleine didn't bring anyone to cut him off he'd never forgive himself. "I'll take a few weapons with me too."

"Good."

"When are you holding your mating celebration? Kres still seemed averse to the idea."

Vohne smiled. "Next month. The real question is if I should tell my sweet Kreslan before the event or at it."

"You know he's good with a knife," Bleine warned.

"Yes. I like the danger." Vohne laughed.

Bleine shook his head. "I'm glad my mate has a less maniacal personality."

"I prefer to call it assertive," Vohne countered.

"You can call it what you want, but I don't want to be on your mate's bad side. By the way, I wanted to tell you I'm concerned about the prophecy. I need to find the original text."

Vohne frowned. "What are you talking about?"

"I'm working off a translation. The more I study it, the more I'm convinced the wording isn't right. I think somewhere along the way someone misread the original. I need to find it to determine for myself."

"Where do you think it is if it isn't in the main library?" Vohne asked.

Bleine shrugged, frustration rushing through him. "I'm hoping it didn't burn down with the original palace."

Vohne frowned. "That would be a shame. Maybe while you're exploring you can try to see if anything survived."

His brother didn't need to convey how weird it was that no one had ever thought to check before. Definitely magic at work here. The only question was whether the spell was failing, and if so, what would it reveal when it finally broke. A spell lasting for centuries must've had some powerful magic behind it.

"I'll take a look around. You never know what might have survived. The manuscripts I have are very vague and use old text. Our great-grandmother wrote the original and the earliest translation was two hundred years later. According to the priest's words, the solution to all of our problems 'lies in the heart of the Thresl'."

"That's nice and vague," Vohne said dryly.

"Isn't it though?" Bleine asked. The more time he wasted, the higher the chance that Earl would escape. "I'll stop by the armoury then head out. I'm only going to take four guards with me. If I take a huge group he'll hear us coming before we even get close to him."

"Sounds good. Keep me posted and take a communicator with you."

"Will do." Bleine stood and gave his brother a short bow that had Vohne rolling his eyes. "Why don't you spend the day planning your wedding? I can't wait to see what colours you use. Kres strikes me as a flower kind of guy. Make sure you use lots of them."

Laughing at the images building in his head, Bleine left his brother's office and headed off to get some weapons. He avoided going back to his own suite. He didn't want Sarler asking questions if he was awake or to wake him if he was asleep. He'd talk to his mate later. For the first time since they'd bonded, Bleine had a positive feeling when he thought about their relationship.

Chapter Five

Bleine shouldered his pack as he passed the last building that stood between him and the ruins.

"How do you want us, your highness?"

Turning, Bleine regarded the four men who had agreed to accompany him. "Two of you go east, two go west. I'm going to check out the centre section."

One soldier, Dravis, shifted nervously on his feet before speaking in a low, hesitant tone. "Shouldn't someone go with you, sir? I don't mean to be disrespectful, but if Earl sneaks up behind..." He trailed off at Bleine's expression.

"Dravis, I'll be fine." He didn't think it was worth mentioning that no one had got the drop on him in the last two hundred years—the young man already looked embarrassed with having brought up the issue. "I'll call if I see him, before I take chase."

Maybe that would soothe the soldier's conscience.

Dravis looked ridiculously relieved. "Sounds great, Prince Bleine."

The other three soldiers exchanged various expression of disbelief at the gall of the younger soldier. Bleine shook his head at them. He thought it was sweet that the young man was worried enough to speak up.

With a wave of his hand he indicated that the soldiers should spread out as assigned. Not bothering to wait to see if they obeyed, Bleine marched to the centre of the ruins. Torn bits of tape flapped in the breeze where officials had tried to cordon off the unsafe regions. Why they had bothered Bleine didn't know. If anyone was here they knew the condition of the structure. Occasionally they had squatters who tried to set up house in the upper portions of the old castle, but they never stayed for long. Rumours abounded over this part of the city being haunted

The pull to return to Sarler's side burrowed into Bleine like a dull ache, but he refused to give in to the compulsion. Sarler needed his rest, not to have Bleine drooling over him like a puppy in heat.

Missing his mate, Bleine continued his path towards the castle proper. He had just passed the first fallen wall when rubble began to shift beneath his feet.

"Damn." If he fell and snapped his fool neck he wouldn't have to worry about whether Sarler would ever warm up to him. He'd be too dead to be concerned.

Focusing on where he put his feet, he blocked all thoughts of his mate from his mind. He wasn't trying to be childish, but he really needed to focus on where he was walking. A shadowy corner caught his eyes. The remains of a staircase could be seen through the doorway.

Could Earl have gone down the stairs to escape the soldiers chasing him? He might still be there, laughing, thinking everyone was too timid to pursue him.

Bleine's heart beat rapidly, excitement racing through his body. This could be the way downstairs. He wondered how much of the original structure still remained below. A wise man would at least call one of the soldiers to go with him in case part of the building collapsed on him.

He reached for his communicator.

No connection.

The building must be blocking his ability to communicate with the others. He'd just peek inside and see if he could see any signs of anyone passing through. Surely a fast look couldn't do any harm.

Bleine paused in the doorway. Like all Thresls, he had excellent night vision and he could make out dim shapes but not much detail.

"Good thing I brought my light," he murmured softly.

He pulled the small portable light from his pocket and flashed it into the dark corners.

Success!

He could see stone steps leading down. Glad he'd brought extra illumination, Bleine headed towards the stairway. He could see bits of a metal railing that had mostly fallen, collapsed or broken from corrosion. A clear footprint left a mark in the crushed stone.

Yes! Earl must've passed by here. It could've been someone else, but the print appeared fresh.

The smell of dust in the air and a strong musty overtone, made Bleine sneeze. He froze and listened carefully for sounds of inhabitants, absently touching the knife he'd strapped to his thigh. He relaxed when no sounds indicated anyone else was nearby.

If Earl was here, he had travelled much farther down. With his light in his right hand and his knife handle gripped in his left, Bleine took careful steps down the crumbling stairs. After traversing each stair, he thoroughly examined the one below. Despite the lack of a railing and the cracks and crumbles of stone, they appeared relatively stable.

Bleine didn't let looks fool him. There was probably more than one set of bones at the bottom from people who'd had a similar theory. However, the footprints continued and so did Blaine. Vohne was going to kill Bleine for not calling for help, but the need to hunt down the man who'd shot his mate had his inner beast roaring for blood.

Halfway down, the stairs disappeared. A gap of at least six feet existed between where Bleine stood and the other side of the staircase. Flashing his light across the gap he saw nothing but crumbled stone far below.

"Crap," Bleine growled. His voice echoed off the walls. He eyed the distance. He could probably jump that, but if he didn't make it, the landing could be horribly ugly.

The chances of him missing that distance were slim and if he were hurt, his brother or maybe even Sarler would be able sense his distress.

He turned off his light and tucked it in his pocket before taking a few steps back. With his stomach fluttering like it planned to grow wings, Bleine ran to the ledge. He pushed off with his right leg as he flung himself across the wide chasm.

The tip of his right shoe caught the opposite ledge. Digging in, Bleine used his momentum to tumble safely to the other side.

"Ooof." The wind rushed out of his lungs as Bleine landed on his stomach. Gravel scraped his chin and rattled his teeth as his face hit the rough surface of crumbling rock.

"Ouch." Taking mental stock of his body, Bleine slowly climbed to his feet. The sound of shattered glass in his pocket had him carefully reaching inside to pull out his smashed light.

"Damn." Luckily, most of the glass had stayed inside the frame. Unfortunately, the bulb had broken. Bleine set the light on the ground. He'd come back and throw it away later.

The slow trail of blood dripping down his neck annoyed him, but he doubted it was life threatening and decided to ignore it. Poking at the wound wouldn't heal it and it would stop on its own soon enough.

Keeping his fingers on the wall to his left to guide him, Bleine carefully continued his downward path. A small bit of sunlight shone through a hole up above, helping his vision. What he saw wasn't inspiring.

"I hope that bastard is down here after all, or that at least I find the library."

If looters had found the library then they had probably destroyed the contents, either by burning the books for heat or vandalising the room. Bleine still couldn't believe it had been completely abandoned without anyone coming down to check for valuables. Of course, Bleine didn't know how he was going to get back up to the surface either.

Finally, after several missteps, he reached the main floor. Mountains of rubble surrounded him and a few hints of clothing caught beneath the stones told him not all the stairs had fallen without consequences.

Bleine wondered if he'd have to call for help to get out of there. Hopefully, there would be a back way he could creep through, maybe an old tunnel that had been overlooked.

Standing in the middle of a cavernous room, Bleine wondered where to start. He couldn't see any more footprints. A few steps later revealed why. Earl lay on his back at the bottom of the stairs. He obviously hadn't made the jump. His neck tilted at an odd angle and his sightless eyes showed Bleine that Earl's soul no longer resided there.

While part of Bleine was pleased at Earl's death, his animal side hated the lack of closure. He had wanted to be the one who took care of Earl's demise, to bring the body of his kill to his mate.

Bleine shook his head clear of that disturbing image. He'd never had as strong a protective streak with any of his other mates, but the thought of Sarler being injured again made him want to wrap Sarler in a protective bubble and surround him with guards. The fact that Sarler wouldn't appreciate that made the idea even more appealing. He liked to ruffle Sarler's feathers and see the cute, disgruntled look he received in return.

"Well, one problem down. Let's see if we can find the library," Bleine muttered to himself.

The silence in the shattered building had an oppressive feel, as if unknown forces were listening to him babble and were waiting for just the right moment to cut into the conversation.

If the same architects who had built the current palace had had a hand in designing the original then maybe he'd have a chance at finding the remains of the library.

A torch on the wall caught his eye. Bleine slid it out of the metal holder mounted to the crumbling stone. A flame sigil carved on the side of the torch base sent a wave of relief through Bleine. He wouldn't have to hunt down a lighter.

Bleine brushed his thumb across the symbol of fire. "Light," he intoned.

The top of the torch burst into flame.

"At least something still works around here," Bleine muttered. Hopefully there weren't any gases escaping. Right now his biggest concern was tripping and breaking an ankle on the rocks. Lifting the torch to get a better view, Bleine spotted two openings up ahead. Both had some rubble blocking the way but appeared passable.

"I hope this castle is smaller than ours," Bleine whispered. He didn't want to have to come back over and over again, heedlessly searching for a lost room that had probably disappeared or succumbed to demolition centuries ago. If it turned out to be a multiple trip project, he would bring soldiers next time to build a bridge across the broken stairs. No way would he chance that jump over and over again, especially if he wanted to haul things out.

Bleine glanced down each hallway but couldn't see much from where he stood. One side didn't appear any more tempting than the other in his limited torchlight.

"I guess I'll go left." The sound of his own voice in the hushed darkness reassured him some. If there were any people living down here, they were quieter than mice. In fact, now that he thought about it, he hadn't run across any vermin or animals of any kind. Strange. He'd have thought the little creatures would've taken advantage of the ruins.

The air, stale and musty, made Bleine sneeze. Nothing moved, rustled or startled at the sound, just more silence.

"Yeah, this isn't creepy," Bleine said dryly.

As he walked down the hall, the first door he peeked inside had nothing but a heavy coating of dirt and a caved in ceiling. Broken stone, shattered wood and burnt remains of the fire that destroyed the palace continued to meet Bleine's gaze as he went from room to room. He had almost given up when he reached a side corridor that revealed another staircase heading down.

He wondered how deep the castle went into the earth. They had been unable to discover any blueprints of the original palace. No one currently alive had ever set foot in the structure. The inhabitants from before had either died in the original palace fire or in the Great Purge.

The lack of knowledge in a culture where history was revered struck a strange chord with Bleine. He didn't understand how such a large portion of their past had literally been erased, first with fire, then with ignorance.

Clutching the torch tightly in his fist, Bleine traversed the narrow staircase. This one, built of wood, had miraculously survived both rot and flame.

The floor below had none of the debris of the upper levels. No rubble, no soot and, oddly enough, barely any specks of dust coated the ground. It almost appeared as if someone was maintaining this area.

Nerves on edge, Bleine touched the handle of his knife for reassurance. It wouldn't protect him against a large threat but could be the difference between getting away from whatever might be living down here and not surviving at all. He'd anticipated confronting Earl on his own, but this was an entirely different situation. He could take one man but not countless enemies.

A half a dozen closed doors were in his immediate circle of light. He sensed the corridor went deeper into the belly of the palace. These must've been used as storage or prison holds, he couldn't tell which.

The first door hung off its hinges as if a large animal had ripped it apart. Claw marks, much larger than any Thresl paw Bleine had ever seen, crossed the front of the door like a warning. Bleine hoped a beast with a claw print that large didn't still lurk the halls. Bleine's knife would be a mere pinprick against such a creature.

He hesitated but for only a moment. He might not be as bold as his brother, but he had determination on his side. He needed to find those books. They might help guide Vohne towards the best future for their people. Their great-grandmother Elisa, human bondmate to their great-grandfather, had seen many things with her powers and had taken copious notes. Most of her journals had been lost through the years. Bleine suspected they had been left in the library. Why their father wouldn't have gone to retrieve them but had saved the translations Bleine didn't know, and since Father wasn't there to ask, they would have to find their own answers.

Stepping into the room, Bleine lifted the torch high to look around. A large bed squatted in the middle of the room. Something dark covered the surface. Curiosity had Bleine stepping closer.

A thick layer of black fur coated the comforter.

"What in the gods did this?"

Surely nothing lived down here. A low growl had Bleine spinning around. He pulled out his knife and crouched, ready for an attack.

Nothing.

Sweeping his torch left and right, he searched for any occupant.

Still nothing.

While still keeping an eye out for danger, Bleine peeked into the closet. The wardrobe was empty. Bleine checked around the room, but there weren't any other doors, probably because the palace had had no private baths in that era. Instead, there had been large pools for bathing and outhouses that had vanished long ago.

Bleine stepped back outside the room. Looking both ways down the hall, he didn't see anything to match the noise he'd heard.

"Hello," he called out. Feeling like an idiot who was jumping at shadows, Bleine headed for the next room. Of course, if there was anyone else there he might as well have placed a big sign stating 'come get me' on his chest.

Another growl, this one louder.

There. He'd definitely heard something.

Bleine spun around. "Oh, fuck."

He almost dropped the torch as the biggest Thresl he'd ever seen soundlessly crept forward. No doubt lived in his mind that this beast had been responsible for the scratched door he'd seen.

"Hey, buddy." Bleine tried to use his most soothing voice as he wondered where this Thresl had come from. Did it have any sense of awareness or was it completely a beast? He'd heard of some Thresls becoming feral if they didn't find their mate. His heart almost forgot to beat at the thought of having to combat this monster on his own. He'd never mock Vohne for his protectiveness again. He was a foolish, foolish, prince to have come down here alone.

The menacing noise emitting from the creature had Bleine stepping back in slow, careful motions, making sure not to do anything quickly that might startle the animal.

"Easy, fellow. I mean you no harm."

"You trapped me here."

The voice in his mind was deep and full of power. The words echoed in his head.

"What? I didn't trap you here. I just came to find the library and search for someone." Bleine wondered if the creature had gone mad confined down below. Maybe it had fallen down the stairs and couldn't find a way back up. Bleine didn't remember hearing of any missing Thresls, but it might not have necessarily been brought to his attention.

The Thresl stepped closer, sniffing the air as if trying to catch Bleine's scent. Bleine froze in place. He might have Thresl blood, but he'd never seen one this large. Even Vohne hadn't come to Bleine's shoulder in Thresl form the few times he'd seen his brother before his change.

"Broken."

The word filtered into Bleine's mind.

"You're broken?" Bleine scanned the Thresl but didn't see anything wrong with it, despite its frightening size. The beast continued to stare at Bleine until he realised what the creature meant. "I'm not broken," Bleine protested. If anything, Earl was broken.

"You have lost your beast," the large cat proclaimed.

"I haven't lost it. I transformed. Everyone loses their cat when they become human," Bleine snapped. He could still feel his animal self beneath the surface. Sometimes it was downright maddening.

"I can give it back to you," the Thresl promised.

"That is impossible." If there had been a way to do that, someone would've shared it years ago.

"You are not like the others. You can be taught...if I don't kill you first." The Thresl sat on its haunches and licked its paw. It watched Bleine with its cold amber eyes.

"I'd prefer if you didn't," Bleine said. He was pleased that his voice sounded calm even though his nerves were jittery. His weapons wouldn't do much against such a large beast. It would be like trying to take down a spaceship with a dart gun.

"We'll see."

The cat didn't seem in a hurry to end his life, so Bleine tried to stay casual even as sweat pooled at the base of his spine. The Thresl could probably smell the stench of his fear but there wasn't a whole lot he could do about that.

Bleine didn't make any sudden movements, unsure what to do next. Surely if there were a library, this inhabitant would know its location. But he didn't want to move forward and startle the beast while it was contemplating whether to kill him or not.

"Come with me," the Thresl commanded.

Bleine bit back his objection. After all, this wasn't his home. His family might have owned it centuries back, but it plainly had been this creature's residence for a while.

He followed the Thresl's path down the hall, wondering if the beast's eyes had adapted after living so long in the dark. Even Bleine's Thresl vision couldn't make sense out of the complete blackness surrounding them. His torchlight didn't extend more than a few feet ahead of him.

After walking for several minutes, the Thresl stopped in front of a pair of double doors. With a quick glance at Bleine, he went to his hind legs and pushed the doors open with its paws. Bleine quickly followed the Thresl.

Holding the torch higher, Bleine gasped as he took in the walls of books covering every vertical surface.

"I believe this is what you were looking for?"

Bleine nodded. "Yes it is. How did you know?"

The Thresl snorted. *"I can easily read your mind, Bleine, son of my deceitful brother. My mate named me Saintaron before your father killed him, left me to die and set the palace on fire. You can call me Saint."*

Bleine's mouth dropped open. "What are you talking about? The palace fire was an accident. It happened hundreds of years ago." At least that was how he'd always heard the story. Of course, his father was the one who had told him. Would the king have confessed if he'd set the palace ablaze himself? Why would he want to? Surely his father would never endanger people in such a way…or would he? Bleine had known his father had had a ruthless streak but destroying his own brother…?

"Where is your father?" Saint asked. *"I expected him to come back for me, to gloat if nothing else. I'm surprised it took one of your blood so long to check on me. Sloppy of him not to make sure I died."*

"He's dead. My mother died giving birth to my sister and my father died with her," Bleine said.

"I am sorry to hear about your mother. Her only flaw was loving your sire. I should kill you now and take back the throne that your father stole from me."

Bleine stepped away from the beast. Apparently he'd let his guard down too soon. "First of all, I'm not the king. And how do you plan to get out of here anyway?"

If leaving the castle were so easy Bleine figured Saint would've found a way out of there before now.

Saint snarled, revealing teeth almost the size of the knife at his hip.

"I can only be freed by the one true king. A spell was cast on this palace to kill anyone entering unless they were of your father's bloodline. Your father didn't want others investigating his crimes."

That explained the lack of looters. "Why would my father try to destroy you?"

Bleine searched his mind but he couldn't remember any instance where his father had even mentioned he'd had a brother. It was as if the king had erased an entire portion of his family. The man Bleine had known as his sire hadn't been exactly warm and fuzzy, but Bleine would've never pegged him for fratricide.

"I discovered he'd been selling off the royal jewels to finance his own projects. He'd become obsessed with our grandmother's writings and was determined to be the king who reincarnated. He figured if he killed me he would take my place. Unfortunately for him, I didn't die, and from what you said, he didn't reincarnate."

Satisfaction oozed from the beast. Apparently a grudge nursed for centuries didn't vanish overnight.

"If you're looking for revenge, my father's dead and I'm not going to take you to my brother. He's the true king and I'll let you kill me before I let that happen." He sent a silent apology to Sarler. At least the human half survived the death of a Thresl pairing. Maybe not happily, but Bleine's demise wouldn't kill Sarler.

Saint stared at Bleine with his cool gold eyes. *"How did my traitorous brother raise such a loyal son? You would truly give up your life for your brother?"*

"I have done many things for the sake of Vohne and I will continue to protect him. If I have to die down here in order to keep you from him, I will." Bleine's heart raced as he contemplated his own death.

"Hmm." Saint examined Bleine as if he were a strange creature he'd never seen before. *"I like you."*

"Umm, thanks." Hope lifted his spirits momentarily.

"It's a shame I'll probably have to kill you," the beast mused.

"Yeah, I'm not really thrilled about it either. How did you survive all these years?" Bleine asked trying to divert the creature from his determination to kill him.

"Magic. The same magic that traps me here keeps me alive. From what I can tell, when your father set the spell to prevent anyone from finding this place, he accidentally froze time around it. Which is why this section has remained relatively unscathed."

"Would it kill you to leave?" Bleine asked worriedly.

Saint growled. *"I don't know. It just doesn't let me. I can't push through the spell. It shoves me back. Though, since you were able to come in you might have weakened the magic. At this point I would welcome my own death. The life I have lived isn't worth having. I've learnt secrets few Thresls know, but I am sick of seeing only my own shadow."*

"What secrets?"

"That humans are meant to assist us not define us. I know how to break the link between human and Thresl in a way that leaves both parties unharmed. I learnt how to return to my Thresl form, which prevented me from dying at the loss of my mate."

Saint's gold eyes dimmed at the memory.

"How can that be? Were the purists right? All those pointless deaths." Horror filled Bleine as he remembered the painful ripping when both his mates had died.

"What purists?"

Bleine walked over to the table and sat down. He couldn't believe what he was hearing. In halting words, he explained about the purists and how they'd killed thousands of bonded in the Great Purge.

Saint sat down on the floor beside him.

"That's horrible. What did your great king do about this?"

"Nothing. He was prevented from finding his bonded by magic and missed the war." Bleine's throat tightened as visions of dead humans bleeding in the streets flashed before his eyes. They still haunted his dreams when he slept. "I wasn't meant to be king."

"Hey." A large paw patted his shoulder. *"I'm sure you did what you could."*

"Not enough," Bleine whispered. "I couldn't save them all."

Saint's eyes held understanding and compassion in their gold depths. *"It isn't easy leading people. I would like to meet this brother of yours, the one capable of gaining such loyalty."*

Bleine shook his head. "You'll kill him. I can't let that happen."

As much as he wanted to save Saint from his lonely solitude, Bleine wouldn't endanger his brother. He'd just got Vohne back. His wish to rescue Saint from the injustice done against him warred with Bleine's devotion to his brother and king.

"I wish to speak to him. You could bring him down here if you don't trust me."

Bleine laughed. "His bonded wouldn't allow Vohne to endanger himself."

"He'd let a human stop him?" Surprise filtered across their mental link.

"His mate is very protective." Bleine said diplomatically. His gaze wandered around the shelves. "I'm looking for my great-grandmother's journals."

Saint raised an eyebrow. *"The seer? Why do you think they're here?"*

"Vohne found a note from our father mentioning the old library. Since we couldn't find them elsewhere, we thought we'd look for them here."

Saint shook his head. *"I've read everything and her journals aren't here."*

Bleine rubbed his face with his palms in frustration. "I don't know what to do now. All the journals claim this is Vohne's last resurrection. Our enemies are plotting against us and I'm trying to find out what Great-grandmother might have written. The people who interpreted her journals had differing opinions."

"I could help you with that," Saint offered. *"I read them when I was younger. I don't know what happened to them afterwards, but I have them all memorised. I have an excellent memory."*

"So does Vohne, but Great-grandmother's writings were somehow erased from the group memory." His brother retained the memory of the entire Thresl society in his brain, but this last resurrection had been flawed due to a sorcerer's spells. If Saint knew the real writings, he could be invaluable. However, Bleine didn't know if he could trust the man claiming to be his uncle. He could be telling Bleine what he wanted to hear in order to be freed.

Saint sighed. *"The spell that locked me in here took away my ability to feel the others. I lost my mate, my throne and my people all in one day."*

"Because of my father?" Bleine still couldn't imagine that level of cruelty.

"Yes. He wanted to be king. He must've known your brother would be the true king at his birth. I'm surprised he didn't kill him."

Bleine thought back to some of the accidents Vohne had narrowly escaped in their childhood. If he hadn't been faster and stronger than the other Thresls, Bleine doubted Vohne would've made it to maturity.

"I think he might have tried," Bleine mused. He examined Saint carefully. "I know that Vohne can break a bonding link, but the Thresl has to be put in a cryogenic chamber to prevent madness or death. How is it you were able to survive?"

"Maybe I really am insane and no one was around to tell me."

Bleine knew he'd go crazy if he were trapped underground for centuries with no companionship. "But you returned to your Thresl form? I've lost two mates and I've never regressed."

"It's not regression. I retain complete memories. You have lost your way because no one showed you how to transform back. I can show you. Once I am above the surface I will need to re-bond but it won't be because I will die or go insane. I will just ache for my other half. Not pleasant but not deadly."

"But how do you do that?

Saint's sharp eyes narrowed. *"Why? You must be bonded if you are in human form."*

Bleine explained the situation. "I think he'd be better off without our bonding. If you can show me how to break it and set him free, maybe he can go off and have a normal life."

"But you would always know you were missing a piece of yourself. If he is truly the right one for you then setting him free would be cruel, not a blessing." The big Thresl's tone in Bleine's head indicated he thought Bleine was an idiot.

Bleine shrugged. "I would rather release the man of my heart than have him hate me."

"I've only known you a brief while, but you don't seem like a selfish person. You should talk to him before you make this final step. I will show you how to shift back to your cat self because I don't think anyone should have to give up their other nature. However, before you make any permanent changes in your bond, you should talk to your mate. I know from experience that even if you can feel your mate's emotions, you can't always know what's going on in their minds."

Bleine wondered when the beast had gone from potential murderer to advisor. He wasn't sure he appreciated the change.

Sighing, Bleine set his chin in his hands. "My first mate was a female. She was like sunshine, bright and warm. My second mate wanted me for my kingdom and to kill my brother. I let the soldiers kill her rather than lose him again. Now I'm bonded with a man. I'm hoping we can work things out, but I'd rather let him go then fight every day to be accepted."

He wouldn't be a burden to Sarler every day of his life. Even though Sarler had said he was willing to give their relationship a try, the human hadn't sought Bleine on his own. Bleine would rather suffer and be free than drag Sarler along with him into their relationship.

"Let me show you my ways. We can help each other," Saint coaxed.

Chapter Six

Sarler jolted into a sitting position, gasping for breath.

"What's wrong?" Kres walked over to the bed and took his hand. "Do I need to call a medic?"

"He's gone." Sarler gripped Kres' hand tight until he could feel the bones grinding together beneath his fingers. Panic twisted his stomach in an iron fist. He panted to catch his breath as spots danced before his eyes.

"Who's gone?" Kres asked leaning over and forcing Sarler to meet his eyes.

"Bleine. I don't feel him anymore. It's like our connection was cut." Tears wet his cheeks. He hadn't realised that the warm hum in the back of his head had been Bleine until it had vanished. As much as he'd fought against their bond, he needed it. He craved his connection to his prince.

Kres' eyes glowed for a brief second as if they were powered by electricity. "Vohne says Bleine went to the ruins looking for Earl. Vohne can't get a hold of him.

He's calling the guards that went with Bleine to see what they have to say."

"Okay." Despite Kres' quick action to find out what had gone wrong, he couldn't help thinking this was somehow all his fault. If he'd just accepted his mate as the gift he was, maybe this separation wouldn't have happened. His wounds pulled with his abrupt movement, but he ignored it. The pain was minor compared to the sinking feeling in his stomach. Nausea swirled through him. He took great gulping breaths to calm himself. Something must've happened to Bleine, something bad.

He saw Kres close his eyes and he knew he was talking to Vohne again.

"Any word?"

"The guards who were searching for Earl with Bleine say he's missing. Vohne is heading for the ruins to see if he can sense him. I've got to go."

"C-can he break the bond without my permission?" Sarler wondered how angry Bleine had been at him. He'd thought they'd agreed to work things out between them, but maybe Bleine had reconsidered. Worry increased the pain in his chest. Would the prince be able to survive a third bonding break? Considering how strong Bleine had been so far, Sarler thought he probably could. "Have them check out the cryo chambers too."

Kres rolled his eyes. "He didn't go back in the chambers. They are carefully monitored and Vohne would've told me if Bleine became a princesicle again."

Sarler laughed even though he didn't feel much amusement. "I suppose."

"I know."

Kres had a sexy confidence about him. Sarler could see why the king was so enamoured with his mate.

Sarler's wounds were down to a deep ache. The medics came and gave him healing shots and laser therapy every few hours. In a couple of days he probably wouldn't even see the wounds anymore. The inner healing would take longer to recover from, but the lack of bond with Bleine made the entire situation unbearable.

Sarler didn't want to lie in bed and fuss. He wanted to get up and look for his Thresl. Before, when he'd thought to escape their bond, he hadn't realised how that would feel. No way would he give up the closeness. Not now, not when he'd just figured out how much the prince meant to him.

"I really like him," Sarler confessed.

Kres raised an eyebrow at him. "Yeah?"

The thought of lying naked next to Bleine didn't freak him out or make him think less of himself. On his home planet they still stoned men who loved men. A lifetime of conditioning couldn't be wiped away with one bonding kiss, even if it had been pretty spectacular.

"They kill gays on my home world," Sarler blurted out, hoping Kres would understand his reticence. "I spent my formative years thinking men who loved men were cursed by the gods." He laughed, but it held no amusement.

Kres remained quiet, letting him talk.

"I was really horrified when you bonded me to Bleine. I mean, after that kiss." Heat poured through Sarler as he remembered the sensation of Bleine's lips on his. He longed to feel Bleine's breath against his lips again or Bleine's strong body wrapped around him when he slept.

Yearning for someone and wanting to spend the rest of his life with someone weren't necessarily the same. Except, now, with this man, they were.

"Is that why you don't want to be Bleine's mate?" Kres raised his hand as if to stop Sarler's answer. "Not that I would encourage anyone to mate with a royal, but Bleine's a good guy even if he isn't common folk."

"Says the man bonded with the king," Sarler said dryly.

"Kres would rather be bonded to the sword polisher," Vohne said from the doorway.

From the wide smile crossing Kres' lips, Sarler doubted Vohne's words. Even he could tell Kres was madly in love with his king.

"He does have nice hair," Kres prodded his mate.

Vohne smirked. "Not as nice as mine."

Kres shrugged but didn't deny the statement.

Sarler resisted the urge to scream. How could they banter when his mate was missing? "Have you seen your brother?"

Vohne shook his head. "Last anyone saw him he had left the castle. I think he went into the old castle ruins without backup. I told him to take a guard with him but it appears he left them behind. He never was good at listening."

Sarler thought Bleine listened too well to the wrong things. "I'm sure Kres told you I can't feel Bleine anymore. Is it dangerous to visit the ruins?"

He'd heard some people talking about the ruins as a cool place to hike around but that going inside was too dangerous. People who went in apparently never came back out. Wouldn't death be the only thing capable of severing the bond without kingly intervention?

Vohne agreed. "If you lost contact, either Bleine is seriously injured or there is something preventing your bond. Either way, we need to find my brother."

Sarler bit his lip as he thought of the pain Bleine could be suffering. The prince could be curled up somewhere in the ruins dying because he'd lost connection with his bonded.

"I want to help," Sarler said. What he could do when he couldn't even leave the bed he didn't know, but he didn't like being in the dark when his mate was somewhere out there.

His mate.

Until now he'd sort of considered himself a stand in for whomever Bleine should really be with. He needed to change his thinking. *He* was the prince's bonded and it was his duty to look after his man.

Sarler sat up, hissing as pain sliced through his body.

"Hey, easy." Kres put a hand on Sarler's shoulder and helped him back down. "I know you want to find Bleine, but you've got to rest."

"He could be hurt," Sarler explained. He tried to convey with his eyes the words he couldn't say. He didn't want to mention that Bleine could be dead. After all, Thresls bonded until death. If the prince's death freed Sarler from their bond, he'd never forgive himself.

* * * *

"If I let you leave here will you tell your brother about me?" Saint asked.

They'd been sitting in the library discussing politics. Saint had been fascinated about current court life and the deceptions being played out.

"I haven't decided yet." He didn't want to give Saint false hope, but he knew if he told Vohne about their uncle, he'd come down to see Saint and might get killed in the process. If the stairs didn't finish him off, the giant Thresl might.

"What were they planning?" Bleine asked, curious over what would be so compelling a reason to keep a king contained even onto death.

"*Who?*"

"My father. What was he planning besides taking over the throne?" Bleine still wasn't completely convinced his father would have gone to such lengths to contain his brother. Killing him accidentally would've been easier and less time consuming. It was almost as if he wanted his brother to suffer as much as possible.

"*Your father was involved in Thresl trafficking in order to pay off his debts to his off-world gambling buddies. No one on this planet would take his marker anymore since I refused to pay, and apparently others were willing to work with him in order to get Thresls. The human halves offered ways to sell the Thresls to their home worlds. They thought they could make money off of us.*" Contempt rolled through the voice in Bleine's head.

Bleine swallowed the bile rising in his throat as he realised his father's plans had come to fruition. "They did. We send Thresls off planet to try to find their mates. Our kind are placed with many government agencies and have a great deal of influence across the galaxy." Bleine's stomach curdled at the thought of Thresls as little more than slaves. "They aren't forced to be with anyone. A Thresl can choose not to bond."

"*Not if they are tortured or given the right spell or drugs,*" Saint remarked.

216

Bleine rubbed his hands up and down his arms. This conversation chilled him. "We vet every request," he argued.

"Who does? You personally?"

"No. We have a department who does that," Bleine confessed.

"Are any of the people in that department human?" Saint asked.

"Of course." Thresls and their humans tended to want to work together. The closeness helped their bond. Bleine wondered if maybe that was one of the reasons he and Sarler didn't get along as well. Bleine didn't spend every day beside his mate. He had too much distance between them. He'd have to fix that when he got back…if he made it back.

"I would investigate their procedures if I were you. If they have been hiding their true purpose for hundreds of years, chances are they have grown lax and cracks will show if you probe deeper."

Bleine hated that Saint was probably right. If Thresls had been sold for the past century then Bleine only had himself to blame. He should've paid better attention. Even with a war on, he should've watched out for his people. He'd have to tell Vohne how they'd let their people down. He didn't relish that conversation.

"I've got to get back to Vohne. Tell him what I've learnt."

Despite what Saint had said, Bleine still took the time to search the library. He couldn't trust the word of a beast he had just met. However, after three hours of looking, he was pretty sure Saint was telling the truth.

"I told you they weren't here." Apparently being an all-wise Thresl didn't prevent the smug 'I told you so'.

Bleine barely resisted the urge to bang his head against the wall. "I was hoping you'd overlooked them."

The look he received spoke volumes. Bleine gave a ragged laugh. "Sorry. After all your time here, you probably have all the library books memorised."

"*Yes, I do,*" Saint agreed.

"I'm tired," Bleine said, sitting down again.

"*Your father might have burned them to keep them out of anyone's hands.*"

"But why would he keep the translations?" Bleine asked.

Saint shrugged. "*Maybe he didn't know about them. He was never much of a scholar. Or they were so wrong they amused him.*"

That was an understatement. Bleine was beginning to wonder if maybe their mother had stashed the books in the castle library and Bleine had just missed them. He'd do a renewed search when he got back home.

"*If it makes you feel any better, they were pretty obscure. I can look at the translations and tell you if they are right or not.*" Saint's eyes glittered and Bleine knew his uncle would do anything to get out of his magical prison.

Bleine sighed. "I wish I could trust you."

"*I can teach you how to turn back into your Thresl form,*" Saint offered.

Temptation poked at Bleine. The thought of having the ability to change back and forth excited him.

"I won't be stuck like that?" he asked. Just because Saint could transfer back into his Thresl form didn't mean Bleine could turn back. He had a feeling Saint had abilities long forgotten by most Thresls.

"*Of course not. You've always had the power to go between. You've just forgotten. As I am mateless, I cannot*" *become human again, but you have someone grounding you,"* Saint said.

Bleine took a deep breath. Excitement made his hands shake. "I'd really like that."

Maybe he could completely break with Sarler if he could go back in his cat form. Surely Vohne would grant him a permanent break if he could prove it wouldn't kill him. He wouldn't mind being a beast for a while until he found someone who truly wanted him.

"You will still need a mate but it won't kill you if you are apart. A Thresl can hide for a long time in cat form. I should know," Saint said.

"Can you read my mind?" Bleine stared at Saint in awe. He certainly hadn't voiced his concerns out loud.

Saint lifted an eyebrow. *"I have abilities far surpassing most of Thresl kind. I have had nothing to entertain me for centuries. During that time I've developed my skills. I have much I can show your king."*

Bleine sighed. He didn't know the right thing to do. "What were humans supposed to be to us?" Bleine asked.

"Humans are the heart of the Thresl. We are the soul. Combined we make a solid partnership. If half of the partner dies, you should automatically shift back into your cat form to heal."

"But we don't," Bleine denied.

"Yes. That is strange," the Thresl agreed.

Bleine sighed in frustration. Somewhere along the way, someone or someones had changed the Thresl makeup. Bleine worried if humans were responsible and word got out, they'd have a second Great Purge.

"You must tread carefully. If someone has done this they have been working in stealth for centuries. It speaks of someone powerful and patient."

Bleine searched his mind for anyone who met those criteria. He drew a blank.

"I can't think of anyone who would be capable of doing such a thing. There aren't any more contenders for the throne."

"These kinds of people prefer to be the power behind the figurehead. Find out who is trying to get close to your brother. Who has the most to gain? Those that are visible often have silent support from the others."

Bleine nodded. "I will look into it when I get back."

How effective he'd be was another matter. He'd been searching since Vohne had returned to find any connection between those who'd prevented Vohne from resurrecting and what they knew of their opposition. He'd turned up little.

"You need to get me out of here."

"I'm still not sure that is the wisest choice," Bleine said. Torn between doing what was right and protecting his brother, he didn't know what to do.

"I could kill you, princeling, and then it wouldn't matter what was in those books." The Thresl's patience had ended. He bared his enormous teeth at Bleine.

"Take another step towards my brother and I'll end you," Vohne spoke from behind Bleine.

Relief swept through him. Thank the gods his brother had come to the rescue. Now they both had to get out of here without anyone getting killed.

"Took you long enough," Bleine teased.

"I had to figure out where you wandered off to and then I had to convince Kres to let me come."

"Your human has you by a tight leash," the Thresl taunted.

Vohne laughed. "You have no idea. If he thought he could get away with a choke chain, he'd snap one on me."

The Thresl tilted his head as he examined Vohne. The king stared him down with little concern showing on his face.

"You do not fear me."

"No," Vohne agreed.

"I could kill you both."

Vohne shook his head. "If you killed us, you'd be trapped here for eternity, and if you harm my brother, I will cut out your heart and bury it."

Bleine frowned over his brother's detailed description. "Why?"

"It's standard Thresl-killing procedure, to make sure he doesn't resurrect," Vohne said with a shrug. "I found it in three different journals."

"Huh."

"You are a worthy king."

"Thank you." Vohne bowed.

"I must be released to help you in your rule. My grandmother had foreseen your demise at the hand of one close to you. Maybe your lover or your brother."

The Thresl gave Bleine a sly look.

A chill went through Bleine. "Wait, if you knew what she wrote, why do you want to help me find the books?"

"Would you have believed me?"

"No." Bleine had to admit before he wouldn't have believed anything a half mad Thresl told him. Now he suspected Saint was smarted than all of them combined. "Can we really go back to animals and keep our minds?"

"Yes."

"Wait, we can turn back into cats?" Vohne asked.

"I will show you and you will set me free," Saint promised.

"What will you do when you get free?" Vohne examined the Thresl carefully. Bleine wondered what his brother saw when he looked at the big beast. Could he feel the loneliness and despair?

"I will seek my mate."

"I thought you said we could do without our mates?" Bleine asked.

"After so many years in solitude, I need companionship. Humans are simple and easily persuaded."

Vohne laughed. "That's because you haven't met my mate."

"How did you find me?" Bleine asked his brother.

"I figured since you weren't in our library and Sarler couldn't feel you anymore, you must've gone into the palace. And since I told you not to come down here, it was pretty easy to determine where you'd gone. It was harder convincing my mate to stay behind."

Looking over Vohne's shoulder, Bleine couldn't hide his grin. "I think you might've failed that challenge."

Vohne turned around. "Hi, honey."

"How did you get down here?"

Kres tilted his head at the Thresl. "It's like I can almost hear him talking. Is he dangerous?"

"Yes." Vohne grabbed Kres' hand as he reached for his knife. "Your knife isn't going to hurt him."

"It will if I drive it through his skull," Kres said practically.

"I like him." The Thresl purred. *"He's willing to get the job done."* Saint's eyes glowed with admiration as he stepped closer to Kres.

Vohne pushed his mate behind him. "Find your own human," he growled.

Amusement trickled through Bleine's mind.

"He's worth protecting. I hope to find one just as good for me. Can we go? The spell must be weakening if your mate can get through. I will be able to leave on my own now."

Bleine realised the choice had been taken from them. Even if they left, the Thresl could probably now escape. With him and Vohne breaking through the spell's seal, they must've caused a rift. As none of them knew magic, they couldn't exactly re-assert the binding.

"We might as well," Bleine said out loud for Kres' benefit. "The question is, how do we get out of here?"

"There's a tunnel," the Thresl purred. "It should be clear now."

Chapter Seven

Sarler knew the second Bleine came closer. Their bond snapped together like puzzle pieces interlocking. Suddenly all the rough edges and ragged temper smoothed over and he became complete.

Tears welled in his eyes. Since the moment he had left the security of his home planet he'd never felt at ease. With Bleine returning, he now knew what he'd been looking for this entire time. He tried to get his wildly beating heart back under control as their bond shifted and wiggled like a living creature between them.

Taking a deep breath, he sent affection back through their shared bond. A jolt of surprise was returned, Bleine having no idea how much Sarler's attitude had changed during their brief separation. Sarler had been unsure over their connection before, but now after even a short time apart he needed Bleine. Craved the man like an addict needed drugs.

"Come to me." Sarler sent the words towards Bleine, hoping his mate would receive the message. Kres had told him he could communicate that way with Vohne,

but they had a different level of bonding. Sarler hoped eventually he could reach that stage with Bleine. If nothing else, he hoped they could become friends as well as lovers.

Just the thought of touching Bleine's hard body, of skimming his hands over Bleine's soft, naked skin, sent shivers through Sarler.

"You called?" Bleine, dusty and tired, approached Sarler's bed.

"What happened? Where were you? I couldn't feel you anymore." The stress of the last few hours swamped Sarler and combined with the pain from his wounds. He burst into tears.

"Oh, sweetness." Bleine kicked off his shoes and climbed into bed with Sarler. "Don't cry. I thought you'd be happy to be rid of me."

Sarler gave Bleine's arm a half-hearted punch. "You're an idiot."

Bleine frowned down at him and damn if he didn't look good doing that too. "But you never really wanted our bond. I thought you'd be happy if we were apart. I'm going to learn how to shift back into my animal form. Apparently the stress is less and you could go back to having someone you really wanted."

"Forget it," Sarler sniffled. "Why couldn't I feel you? When you vanished, I hated it."

Bleine cuddled Sarler closer and told him everything that had transpired in his absence.

"Earl is dead?"

"Yes. He can't hurt you anymore." Bleine kissed Sarler's forehead as if soothing a scared child. Sarler barely resisted the urge to pinch him.

"And you brought back an uncle who can show you some magic tricks and learnt your father was an asshole of epic proportions?"

"Pretty much. At least that's Saint's version of the story. Unfortunately our father isn't here to verify the story or not."

"Why are you so interested in finding your great-grandmother's journals?" Sarler leant back so he could see Bleine's face. "If you know the future, won't you change it? I mean, what she put down now wouldn't be the same if you knew what was happening. Or what if by finding out the future you change it for the worse?"

"We need to find out if she saw us going to war amongst ourselves again, discover if our enemies will overcome us or at least find out who we are battling against. So many things we just don't know." Frustration filled Bleine's voice.

Sarler could tell how much not knowing ate away at the prince. However he didn't think anyone should know the future and messing with it couldn't bring anything good. Sarler kept silent. He'd just got Bleine back and he didn't want to ruin the tentative truce they had between them.

"How are you feeling?"

Sarler lifted his shirt, exposing his smooth stomach. "The wound is all mended. I still have some internal tearing that needs to heal, but overall I'm doing much better."

Bleine didn't speak. Instead, he kissed him.

Sarler gasped against Bleine's mouth. He hadn't expected the embrace. Bleine had climbed up on the bed to soothe him, not to have sex. The kiss awakened parts of Sarler that had lain dormant since the attack. His cock hardened and pushed against his loose pants, seeking out Bleine.

"I see part of you is happy to see me," Bleine teased.

"All of me is happy to see you," Sarler argued. He couldn't convey how much he'd missed his prince. "Kiss me again."

"Bossy, aren't you?" Bleine said.

Sarler would've responded, but Bleine's lips took away his breath, his thoughts and his will to do anything but lay there and let his mate take control. Sarler fisted Bleine's shirt, keeping the prince close. He wouldn't let Bleine escape again, at least not easily.

Bleine looked down at Sarler's grip. "Are you worried I'm going somewhere?"

"Yes." He didn't bother to explain. Instead, he slid one hand behind Bleine's neck and proceeded to show him everything he knew about kissing...which wasn't much, but he figured he would get points for enthusiasm. If Bleine's moaning was any indication, he was doing pretty well.

Bleine slid his hands to Sarler's waist and moved Sarler until he lay on top of the prince instead of beneath him.

"I don't want to put pressure on your wounds," Bleine explained.

He could feel Bleine's hard erection pressing against him. Their cocks rubbed against each other in a friendly greeting. Sarler sighed at the sensation. How many nights had he dared to dream of having another man pressed to his body? Bleine smelt of pure male with a little dust, nothing off-putting and so much to enjoy.

How had he lived so long without this man?

"Are you certain?"

Bleine's words cut across Sarler's lust. It took him a moment to understand the odd question. "About what?"

"About me. About us." Bleine's gold eyes carried the pain of anticipated rejection, like an abuse victim waiting for that next slap. He'd done this. He'd hurt his strong, vital man with his inconsiderate words.

"Yes. I've always hidden what I wanted," Sarler explained. "But I'm done with that. I want you."

Years of holding back his needs, suppressing the urge to touch another man, were swept away by his longing, by his need to please his mate.

A slow smile crossed Bleine's face. "Good."

There wasn't time for any more words, not with Bleine taking Sarler's mouth as if he were a country to conquer. Sarler relaxed beneath the prince's touch, yielding, giving and offering up anything his mate needed.

"*I am yours,*" Sarler projected.

Bleine bit Sarler's neck. "I know," he said, grinning. "I can feel it along our link."

"You can hear me?" Joy filled him. Surely they were meant to be if their connection was so strong.

"Yes." Bleine kissed him again.

Sarler melted. This was how it was supposed to be. Two people joined in their bond. His parents would've screamed at the sight. That only made it that much better.

Sarler luxuriated in Bleine's touch. The rough tips of the prince's fingers as he slid them beneath Sarler's shirt, the breathy moans he made against Sarler's neck.

"Can I undress you?" Bleine's gold eyes shone with lust and his wet mouth tempted Sarler beyond reason.

"You can do anything you want," Sarler promised.

Bleine's smile warmed Sarler from the inside out. He'd made this serious man happy. From what he'd learnt of the prince, Bleine took the future of his people seriously and had seen and done whatever necessary to see to their future.

All thought vanished when Bleine carefully rolled Sarler onto his back before slipping to the side of the bed and stripping Sarler naked in swift, efficient movements.

"What about you?" Sarler asked when Bleine remained clothed.

"Give me a minute."

However, Bleine showed no rush to undress. Instead, he turned his attention to Sarler's cock. Flushed pink and dripping with excitement, his erection all but waved to get Bleine's attention.

Bleine scooted back between Sarler's thighs and without warning swallowed Sarler in one fast gulp.

"Oh!" Sarler was beyond forming words. His mind went white from overload. Closing his eyes, he became a creature of pure sensation. Never had anything felt so amazing.

A wet finger probed his hole. Sarler widened his legs to allow Bleine access to anything he wanted. His ass clenched as he imagined Bleine's large cock pushing its way inside.

"Easy, love. I won't do anything you're not ready for," Bleine promised.

"Suck me!" Sarler demanded. If Bleine didn't finish his blow job, there would be one less royal in the world. Afterwards he would insist Bleine screw him into the mattress. He could suffer later—right now was for sex.

"Demanding, beautiful boy," Bleine whispered against Sarler's wet skin.

He whimpered. "Please."

That must have been the word to use, because Bleine diligently returned to sucking Sarler's erection into his mouth. "Yes, please yes," Sarler whispered. He grabbed the bed sheets with the same tight grip he'd used on Bleine's shirt before.

Bleine hummed around Sarler's cock.

"I'm coming," Sarler groaned.

Bleine didn't let up. With a gasp, Sarler poured his release down his lover's throat. Exhaustion had spots dancing before his eyes. Before he could say *thank you* or *more* or anything else, Sarler slipped into unconsciousness.

* * * *

The room was dark when Sarler awakened.

"I've never had anyone pass out after a blow job before," Bleine commented.

Sarler grabbed the glass of water sitting on the table beside him and took a drink. "I'm surprised. You give amazing ones."

Bleine laughed. "I'm glad you think so. I haven't had a great deal of practice. How are you feeling? I was worried I overdid it with you."

Sarler carefully took stock of his body. "I'm good," he said with surprise. Even the inner pain seemed muted.

"It's the bond. The more we connect the more of my abilities you'll absorb. You're starting to get enhanced healing abilities."

"That makes sense." Sarler had counselled several bondmates so he knew how it worked in theory. In reality, he had less experience. "Since I'm your third mate will there be less merging?"

A Thresl, when first changed, began to form into his mate's ideal.

Bleine frowned. "I'm not sure. I didn't change at all between my first and second mates. Whether we bond enough to affect me will be interesting to see."

Sarler didn't know if 'interesting' or 'creepy' was the right word. After all, to be responsible for another person's personality and happiness was a big job. To have that power over a prince paralysed him with fear.

"What is it?" Bleine rubbed Sarler's chest. "What's wrong?"

"I don't know if I can be the right person. What if I screw up and you become someone you don't want to be?"

Bleine frowned then kissed Sarler on the cheek. "What are you talking about?"

"I don't know if what I want will be what's best for the kingdom. What if my personality makes you a horrible person?" Sarler blurted out.

Bleine laughed. "You're an empath, love. Somehow I doubt you're going to turn me into a psychotic killer."

"There are several degrees of personality between a good person and hatchet swinger," Sarler said dryly.

"Hmm, I'll have Vohne hide all the swingy weapons. Will that make you feel better?" Bleine's eyes sparkled with amusement.

Sarler sighed. "You're not taking me seriously, are you?"

"When you start to make sense I'll consider it," Bleine promised. "Why don't you get some rest? You're still healing."

Bleine's affection for him soaked into Sarler like warm water surrounding him until he floated on a sea of tenderness. Except...having Bleine that close excited more than soothed him.

Amber Kell

"No. I want to feel you inside me. If we're going to build our connection, we need to be completely bonded. I want you to know I'm committed to our relationship." He grabbed Bleine's wrist before he could move away. "No! This isn't about pity or anything else you are building in your head. It's about me and you, not other people's expectations."

Hope lit up Bleine's eyes. "Really? Because I think I can get us out of this if you are interested."

"I'm not interested. You're stuck with me and I'm not going to let you go."

Bleine's smile was blinding. "Okay."

"Good." Sarler nodded. "I'm glad you got that figured out. Now strip!"

"I see you are going to be a demanding mate," Bleine said in mock sorrow. "I'd best make sure I'm in good shape to become your personal love slave."

"Exactly. You might have to cut back on your princely duties to lay around and wait for me in my bed," Sarler teased, trying to hide his nervousness.

It didn't work. Bleine paused after removing his shirt. "Are you certain? Not about the mating thing, but about the sex. We don't have to rush anything."

The concern on Bleine's face soothed the mild panic trembling through Sarler's body. As if he'd passed an important test, his nerves smoothed out like the calm after a storm. "I've never been more certain of anything in my life," he assured Sarler. "I want you and I want to be yours."

"Good." Bleine stripped off his pants, revealing a beautiful long, thick erection that had Sarler's mouth watering for a taste.

"I want to suck you."

Bleine shook his head. "If your mouth goes anywhere near my dick it will be all over. I'm on edge as it is."

Sarler smiled. The ego boost he'd received from knowing his prince needed him so badly wiped away the rest of his concerns like a wind blowing away spider webs. "How do you want me?"

Bleine tilted his head as he considered the problem. "Normally I'd say on top but moving up and down like that might hurt."

"I'm not feeling much pain right now," Sarler said. "How about I go on my stomach and we put pillows beneath me?"

"Okay but if you start having any kind of pain you tell me immediately. Like I said, we don't have to do this now. We can wait."

"I don't want to wait. I want to belong to you." Sarler needed that connection to know that Bleine saw him as his forever mate. If the prince always had one foot out the door, they would never bond properly.

After an excruciatingly long moment, Bleine nodded his agreement. "But you tell me if you're in pain. I won't continue just so you can show me how strong you are."

"Deal." Unless the pain was excruciating, Sarler would ignore it. Bleine was wrong. He *did* need to prove something to him. He had to prove he was willing to accept his male mate even if they hadn't had the best beginning.

Bleine made sure Sarler was comfortably positioned before he grabbed something out of a drawer.

"I'll make sure you're nice and slick before I do anything. I'll take care of you," Bleine promised.

"I know you will," Sarler said. Bleine meant sexually, but he knew the prince would do whatever was necessary to protect his mate, even out of the bedroom.

A thick finger circled Sarler's hole. He clenched his ass against the intrusion. A soft kiss on his back had him relaxing again. "You need to accept me, love," Bleine said. "It will be harder if you don't relish my touch."

Sarler took slow, deep breaths and the next time Bleine's finger pushed slightly inside his ass he was better prepared.

"That's it. Just let it happen." Liquid dripped down his crack. He wiggled from the sensation.

Bleine's deep chuckle made him smile. "I'm just making sure there's enough lubrication."

Considering his entire ass was probably coated with the stuff, Sarler had to shake his head. "I'm pretty sure there's enough there for six virgins."

"Good thing I'm only interested in one," Bleine said.

The affection in Bleine's voice had Sarler relaxing even further. He tentatively lowered his shields a bit. Adoration poured through him like warm honey, sticking to every bit of him in a sweet coating of love.

When Bleine shoved in a second finger Sarler had no difficulty accepting the intrusion. How could he not want this man who thought of him with such overpowering tenderness? An emotion he more than reciprocated

"Yes, fill me," Sarler urged.

"I will, but I want to be careful."

Sarler pushed back on the prince's fingers. He didn't want careful—he wanted Bleine inside him now.

"Easy, love," Bleine soothed. "I want this first time to be a happy memory."

"It will be because it's you," Sarler assured him.

"Don't say things like that," Bleine groaned. "I'm trying to be good."

"Don't be good. Be bad. Very, very bad," Sarler urged.

Bleine laughed.

The bed dipped as Bleine climbed on the bed behind him then finally, finally the wide, blunt tip of Bleine's cock pressed against his hole. Sarler took long, slow breaths to relax.

"Let me in, love," Bleine whispered, his voice silky soft in the stillness of the room had Sarler ready to promise anything to get his prince inside him. Anything he wanted Sarler would give, anything to hear that voice whispering to him again.

Arching his back, Sarler blocked out the pain and focused on his mate. Bleine's hands gripping Sarler's hips in a touch both commanding and gentle calmed Sarler's nerves.

When Bleine pushed in, he rubbed against something inside Sarler. Sarler jolted at the connection.

"Easy, I've got you."

"Move!" Sarler needed more. He needed Bleine to ease the ache building in his body. He clenched his ass around Bleine's erection, drawing a hiss from his lover.

"If you keep that up it's going to be over before it starts."

"Then stop messing around," Sarler grumbled.

Bleine's laughter puffed across Sarler's ear, sending shivers down his spine. His ears had always been sensitive and Bleine's hot breath didn't help matters.

"Ooh, I think I found a good spot."

Bleine licked the top of Sarler's ear. Sarler moaned. He moaned again when Bleine pumped his hips, sliding in and out with delicious friction.

"R-right there," he gasped foolishly, as if Bleine couldn't tell by the obscene noises ripping out of him like he would die before the next push or pull. Both motions added more sensation on top of the feeling of being stretched and the pure joy pouring from Bleine like liquid happiness.

"I'll give you what you need. Don't worry," Bleine promised.

Sarler had no doubt his mate knew exactly what to do to push him over the edge. Nothing but bliss came from Bleine. No nerves or discomfort or disgust that his partner wasn't female. For the first time all the emotions emanating from another person were positive. So happy were Bleine's vibes that Sarler's heart ached from the joy of it.

Riding on the energy high of bonding with his mate, Sarler came without anyone touching his erection. A sigh parted his lips.

"I can't believe you came without me," Bleine said. Amusement peppered the air. Sarler clenched around Bleine in retaliation. "Oh fuck."

Sarler smiled, wetness spilled inside him and satisfaction not his own rolled through his body. Sarler's cock made a valiant effort to rise again, but he was too relaxed now. With a shudder, he toppled onto the mattress…right into the wet spot he'd created.

Bleine pulled him out of the sticky essence. "Come on, love, let's get washed up."

"Yes, let's," Sarler agreed. He might have enjoyed their encounter, but he hated the mess afterwards.

The shower was quick and almost business-like with their efficiency. Sarler's eyelids dipped down a few times, only to snap open when Bleine rubbed a cloth across his body.

He didn't realise he'd dropped off again until he woke up when Bleine turned off the water.

"Come on, let's get you back to bed."

Bleine must've talked to someone while Sarler had zoned off because different sheets covered the bed and all the sticky spots were gone. Sarler was half asleep as soon as his body went horizontal.

"Get some rest, love. I'm going to go see my brother."

"M'okay," Sarler murmured. Next time he'd make more of a fuss about not getting cuddled right after sex, but Bleine probably had some important things to discuss with the king and Sarler would be able to sense if there was a problem. "Have fun."

Bleine kissed Sarler on the cheek. "I already did."

Chapter Eight

Bleine waited until his mate had completely fallen asleep before leaving their suite.

It was still early evening. Hopefully he could catch Vohne before he hunkered down for the night with his mate. If he was already in his room, Bleine could forget getting his brother's attention. Nothing could pull Vohne from Kres' side, except maybe a natural disaster and even that would not necessarily be enough of a distraction.

Bleine watched the people as he passed. Most of them nodded or bowed. A few watched him with wary gazes that made him wonder what they were thinking. Saint had it easy. At least he could read other people's thoughts. Bleine wondered if he could get the Thresl to help him weed out the dangerous ones in their ranks.

As if he'd heard him thinking of him, and he probably had, the large beast appeared in Bleine's path.

"You're really quick," Bleine said. Despite the fact he knew Saint could read his mind, Bleine spoke out

238

loud. He couldn't quite adjust to knowing words weren't necessary.

"I don't have much to do and all your people are frightened of me," the Thresl explained.

"Are you interested in helping out a bit?"

"Just tell me what you want me to do."

"I need to talk to Vohne get his approval first." Spying on their people was probably ethically wrong, but so was plotting against your king.

"Things went well with your mate." The cat's smug tone had Bleine laughing.

"Things went really well." He wanted to believe Sarler's about-face was real. If Sarler truly had been suppressing his desires for so many years, how could he know that Bleine was what he wanted? Maybe any warm male would do. Shaking off his self-doubt, he decided to focus on the important things right now, like saving a kingdom.

"I could read your mate's intentions if you'd like."

Bleine sighed. "No. That would be cheating. Have you seen Vohne?"

Better to change the subject than come across like an idiot.

"He's in the library."

"Why aren't you with him?"

"I'm hunting. I felt something strange. I wanted to explore."

"Don't scare the crap out of people."

"I won't frighten anyone important."

That non-answer didn't reassure Bleine. With a smug flick of his tail, Saint sauntered down the hall. Bleine resisted the urge to follow. The Thresl deserved some time to explore after having been trapped for centuries.

Bleine found Vohne in the library, sitting at a table with the translation before him. No sign of Kres. Bleine relaxed. If the king-mate wasn't there then Vohne wouldn't be on his way out.

"Find anything new?"

Vohne sighed. "No. I thought maybe I'd overlooked something but no such luck. I think we'll have to discover what's going on the usual way."

"Torture?"

Laughter looked good on Vohne, Bleine decided. This reincarnation of the king had a more solemn side that Bleine thought needed to relax more. The only time Vohne teased was with his mate.

"I'm thinking we move my wedding up. Kres might grumble, but everything's lined up and Saint can attend and scan the crowds. See if he can spot anyone who intends to do us harm."

"How is Kres going to take that?"

Vohne grinned. "Weird. I must have forgotten to mention it."

The brothers laughed together even as Bleine considered how to get a weapon-proof vest beneath Vohne's tuxedo.

"I did find one paragraph I'd overlooked before," Vohne said, frowning at the book open before him.

Bleine leant back in his seat. "What is it?"

Vohne spun the journal around for his brother to see. "The translator wrote that the true king and his mate will be betrayed by the shadowy trio."

"That's nice and non-specific," Bleine drawled.

Vohne ran his fingers through his hair. "We need to prepare for a coup and find Saint a mate. If we have him on our side, we'll have a big advantage. Besides, he can read people's minds. See if you can get him to be your advisor."

Bleine laughed. "I'll talk to him about it. It'll give him something to focus on before he starts trouble just because he's bored."

"Excellent, then all we need to do is finish planning the wedding and hope my mate is still talking to me in order to perform the vows," Vohne said.

"Good luck with that," Bleine offered.

Vohne rolled his eyes. "Thanks. I'm going to need it."

* * * *

Sarler awoke alone. He was used to that by now. His mate tended to wander off. Closing his eyes, he tried to narrow down Bleine's emotional signature. He could almost hear Bleine laughing as he spoke to someone. The warm regard pouring from Bleine made Sarler think the prince was probably with his brother.

Sitting up, he smiled. No pain.

The combination of medics and lovemaking had healed Sarler completely.

Starting to slide out of bed, he froze. The largest Thresl he'd ever seen walked into his room without warning.

"H-hello," Sarler said cautiously.

"You are the prince's mate."

"Yes." He wondered if he should have admitted that to the strange beast.

"I am Saint, your mate's uncle."

"Nice to meet you." It really wasn't. He wanted the giant beast to get the hell out of his bedroom, but he didn't know of a way to say that without insulting his in-law.

Sarler wrapped a robe around his naked body, conscious of the Thresl's amber gaze.

"You will care for him?"

"Yes. Of course."

"He will need you in the time to come. There are those who seek to destroy the royal house. The brothers must stand. They must survive until I can take over."

"I'm not a fighter." Sarler would do whatever he could to protect his mate, but he had only joined the military to get off-planet. The recruiter had got him away from his family and that was all he'd required at the time.

"You must claim your inner warrior and make your stand."

"O-okay." Sarler wondered what more he could do. He'd never been much of a fighter.

"Sometimes the battle for the heart is the hardest one to fight."

Sarler nodded cautiously. "I'm going to go and find Bleine now."

The Thresl stared at Sarler as if the cat could see straight into his soul. Usually he could get a sense of another person when they were near, but this Thresl...man...whatever it was exuded a calm emptiness as if there was nothing inside. As if someone had scooped out all its emotion and left nothing in its place but a worn out beast.

With a final glance at Sarler, the Thresl turned around and left. To Sarler's surprise, the guards didn't leave their posts to check on him. For all they knew, he could've been sliced and diced by the giant Thresl.

Sarler quickly dressed in more appropriate clothes. After opening the door, he peeked outside. The guards looked at him questioningly.

"Where did the Thresl go?" He wanted to make sure the beast wasn't going in the same direction.

"What Thresl?" the guards asked.

"Never mind. I'm going to find Prince Bleine."

The Thresl must know how to disguise his presence, a skill Sarler would love to have. He headed towards Bleine. He could feel his mate's presence getting closer so he knew he was going in the right direction.

After only one wrong turn, he found the right door.

Bleine looked up when he entered. The prince's smile made the walk worth it even if he was low on energy right then. "How's it going?"

"Not a lot of new info. Vohne is going to get married to see if Saint can identify the people plotting against us."

"Oh." Sarler sat down beside Bleine. Bleine's emotions bled around him in a pool of frustration. Sarler thought he'd drown in it. He decided not to mention the strange visit. If they needed Bleine's uncle to save them, then bringing up his concerns about the big cat appearing in his bedroom might send up the wrong signals. "Anything I can do?"

Bleine shrugged. "Stay alert. Pay attention to the grumbles of the court and hope no one goes for an assassination attempt."

"That's not funny." Sarler scowled.

Bleine wrapped his fingers around Sarler's left hand, gripping it lightly. "I appreciate you trying to help. During Vohne and Kres' ceremony, we can mingle and see if you can sense anything odd or anyone who feels as if they are hiding anything. Saint can hunt too and if we come up with anything strange, we'll at least know who to target when we start our investigation."

"I can do that!" A rush of joy went through Sarler. He could help. Some of the frustration of being injured and unable to assist Bleine vanished. He could do this.

He smiled at Bleine, who returned it with a wary look of his own.

"What?" His mate appeared less than excited about Sarler's new assignment.

"Are you sure about this? You are just getting over an attack. I can have guards on you the entire time, but I can't guarantee your safety. We still don't know who is plotting against the crown. I can't have you wandering large crowds unprotected among so many strangers."

"If you expect me to sense anyone, you can't have the guards around me all the time either," Sarler argued. "Their vibes will get in the way of my reading people."

Bleine sighed. "What do you propose then? Because I'm not going to let you mingle with a bunch of people who might not be our allies and who would love to get their hands on a Thresl mate. Everyone knows how much you mean to me and that we'll do anything to get you back."

If Bleine's life didn't hang on the balance of Sarler's actions he'd tease the man about being overprotective. But some things he couldn't kid about.

"You can have them watching me from above. Put them on the balcony and a couple on the perimeter. I can alert them if something goes wrong. I can't have you hanging around me the entire time either. I might not be much of a soldier, but I am trained to protect myself," he reminded Bleine.

"I know. I know. I just don't see you as a big bad fighter. You're more gentle than that."

Sarler gripped Bleine's arm. "I'm not saying I'm ready to go out for combat, but I'm not weak either. I can conceal a weapon on my person for the party. No one would expect me to be armed."

"Good idea," Vohne said approvingly. "We can have a small gun or one of the new laser weapons concealed on you, along with a mic so you can announce if you get into trouble."

"Sounds good." Relief filled Sarler. He wasn't going to be a burden to his mate. He could help. It was as if he was back in school and had got to sit at the popular kids' table. Vohne and Bleine were considering him as a viable option to assist them.

"Why don't you get your mate back to bed, Bleine? He can rest up while I inform Kres we're going to have our ceremony soon. I'll let you know if you need to meet me in the infirmary."

Sarler laughed along with Bleine, but the nervousness emanating from the king laid lie to the laughter. He didn't say anything until they'd left the room.

"Why is the king so nervous about marrying Kres?"

Bleine smiled. "He's not nervous about the bonding. He's nervous Kres will try to find a way out of it."

"Why would he do that? I mean, I know it was postponed once, but surely they aren't going to cancel the entire thing?" From the whispers around the palace, he knew everyone was looking forward to the party. Sarler knew from the history he'd read about the Thresls that mating ceremonies always happened in front of the full court. He couldn't even imagine how bad it would have to be for the king to not present his mate before his people.

"We'll catch them," Sarler vowed. "Or at least find out who's responsible."

"We will, but first we need to strengthen our own bond." Bleine's hot gaze licked across Sarler like a candle flame.

He nodded, unable to speak. Almost without conscious thought his feet moved faster until he was all but running down the corridor back to their room.

Their suite. He liked the sound of that. Of sharing his life with this brave prince who would face down anyone to help his people.

Bleine's footsteps sounded behind him but Sarler didn't stop until he stood at the foot of their bed.

With his eyes locked on Bleine's, Sarler pulled off his shoes, his pants then his shirt in swift, impatient motions. He needed to feel Bleine's hands on him more than he'd ever needed anything in his lifetime.

His desire must've transmitted itself to his mate. Bleine took little time to strip down to nothing. Wrapping a hand into Sarler's hair, he held him still while he plundered his mouth.

A moan escaped his control as Sarler's hard body rubbed against him.

"Let's make sure our bond is well established before we worry about Kres and Vohne," Bleine said.

Sarler nodded at the brilliance of his mate. With a groan, he quickly divested Bleine of clothes. When they were finished for the night, no one would ever again doubt that Bleine and Sarler had consummated their bond.

Epilogue

Bleine had never seen so many people in fancy clothing. Sure, over the centuries he'd seen some version of Vohne marry another version of Kres, but this was the largest group of people ever to attend the ceremony.

Representatives from the surrounding planets and even some far off galaxies were there. It had taken another month before they were able to get everything together for the ceremony. Kres had dug in his heels about inviting a politician he'd gone to Thresl training with. Vohne had refused to let an Admiral attend the event.

By the time all the right people were finally invited, Bleine was ready to throw both of them off a cliff. Luckily, the actual ceremony had gone off without a hitch and Kres now wore a big-ass ring indicating he belonged to Vohne, as if anyone was in any doubt.

As Vohne's closest relative, Bleine was always the one who married him off to Kres. Saint had offered to stand in, but as neither of them knew the Thresl and

Amber Kell

since this might possibly be the last time the couple married, they had politely declined.

"Everyone looks beautiful," Sarler whispered in Bleine's ear. His mate looked stunning in an all-black suit with a gold rose in the lapel, but then he would've thought Sarler amazing in a sack. This was the first time they'd had a chance to exchange more than a few words since the event started.

"You are the only one I see," Bleine replied back.

Sarler blushed. How he could still do that after the hours they'd spent in bed tightening their bond Bleine didn't know.

"Pretty words from a pretty man," Sarler teased. He smoothed Bleine's suit and fixed a strand of Bleine's hair. All the little niceties a couple did for each other.

"Am I all tidy now?" Bleine asked. He had a feeling if Sarler could turn into a Thresl, he would've groomed Bleine with his tongue. The image made Bleine smile. His heart ached with love for the man before him. He'd do anything to keep Sarler safe. "If you feel anything weird you come find me right away. Understand?"

Sarler nodded. "Will do. So far all I can feel is excitement. Everyone is thrilled to be here."

"Good. Hopefully it's because they are excited about the event and not because they think it's the perfect place to attack the king." Bleine scanned the crowd, worry eating away a bit of his excitement.

"Do you think we'll ever have this?"

Bleine turned around at the wistfulness in his mate's tone. "A big ceremony like this where everyone and their second cousin twice removed attends?"

Sarler nodded.

"No." When Sarler dipped his head to hide his expression Bleine slid his fingers beneath Sarler's chin and tilted it back up. "I would never make you stand in front of all these people we don't care about and say your vows. Hell, if Vohne weren't king he wouldn't do it either."

"Oh."

Bleine could see disappointment stayed in Sarler's eyes. "I can see us marrying, but we would only invite people we care about."

Sarler's smile rivalled the sunlight streaming through the windows for brightness. "I'd like that."

"Good. I'd like that too," Bleine confirmed. If Sarler had said he wanted the entire nonsense of hoards of people attending, Bleine would've done that too.

"The people all seem to love your brother."

Bleine turned to see Saint stalking towards them. The people nearest jumped out of the way of the giant beast.

"I do believe you're scaring the guests," Bleine said mildly.

The cat gave a snort of disdain. *"They are unimportant in the scheme of things."*

"You don't sense anyone wanting to do Vohne harm?"

"I read a few people who wanted to take your brother-in-law to bed with them. A few people fantasised about being king, but none of them came across as willing to kill to take the position from him."

Bleine sighed. "So we've learnt nothing."

"Not true," Saint contradicted. *"You learnt your people support their king. If anyone is trying to get the throne now, it is either someone not attending the ceremony or someone off-world."*

Bleine looked around, but he didn't see a lot of people who weren't royalty. Seating was at a premium, so a lot of people didn't get to come. They would have a commonwealth ceremony outside in another couple of months. "I wonder if the people we most need to see are the ones we generally don't invite because of their positions."

"I'm going to walk around a little more," Sarler said.

He could feel something tickling the edges of his subconscious, a waft of animosity like an oily slick across his mind.

"Want me to come?"

"No. I'll be all right."

If he brought the giant Thresl along, he doubted whoever it was would stay put long enough for Sarler to pin them down.

"Be careful, love," Bleine said. A quick kiss was pressed against his lips before his mate wandered away.

Sarler smiled, pleased that his mate trusted him to look into this on his own. He didn't doubt there would be guards watching his every step, but he still appreciated the appearance of independence Bleine gave him.

Straightening his shoulders, he turned and sent out his psychic feelers, tentatively reaching the people he passed.

A cloud of dark energy slammed into his shield.

"Whoa, what was that?" he whispered.

Sarler froze in his spot and spun around until he located the source. A thin man with a cold expression glared at the happy couple. Negativity emanated from the stranger so strongly Sarler was surprised no one else could sense it.

He slowly approached the man.

"Hello."

The man spun to face Sarler as if startled. "What do you want?"

"Is there a problem?" Sarler asked ignoring the man's question for one of his own.

"I knew if I stood here long enough you would appear," the man said, an evil grin crossing his face.

"What?"

"You thought you could escape, didn't you?" A knife appeared in his hand. "Your parents wanted me to give you their regards. They knew you would turn into an abomination. I was just going to kill you, but I think I'll have a little fun first."

The man pressed the sharp blade to Sarler's stomach. "Come with me and I'll spare your mate."

Sarler nodded his agreement.

He couldn't do anything in a room full of people without endangering someone else.

"Head for the exit. I'll be watching you the entire time. Do something stupid and I'll kill you slowly."

Sarler knew the man planned to kill him anyway. He frantically sent mental messages to Saint, hoping the large Thresl was still scanning the room. When he didn't see any sign of the black beast, he knew he was on his own.

Reaching into his pocket, he grabbed the black box. Good thing he'd snatched it out of his other pants this morning. He could feel the stranger's fury. Sarler had thought his parents had forgotten about him by now. He should've known he wouldn't have escaped them so easily.

Without warning, Sarler tossed the box to the floor and smashed it with his heel.

A loud siren pierced the air. Sarler dropped to the floor. He could feel the whoosh of air as the stranger swept his knife across the spot Sarler had stood in.

Out of nowhere the nurse from the medic ward raced behind Sarler's attacker. With an effective kick, she slammed her heel into the man's skull. He tumbled to the ground and didn't get up.

"You all right?" she asked.

"Um, yeah, thanks." Sarler accepted the hand she held out.

Bleine rushed through the crowd and wrapped Sarler in his arms. "Are you all right? Is he one of the betrayers?"

Sarler laughed as relief rushed through him. "No. He was here for me. Apparently my parents weren't happy with my leaving my home world."

"Fuck them," Bleine said. "I'll make sure the representative I send will make it clear that any more attacks on your life will result in war."

"Definitely. You are a member of our family and we don't appreciate attempts on your life," Vohne said, appearing out of the crowd with his arm around Kres. The king motioned for the guards to take the man away. "Who was the lady who saved you?"

"I'll tell you later. It's not a story for a crowded room." Sarler didn't know if the nurse wanted to be exposed to the public. Hell, he didn't even know her name.

"Well, if the fuss is over, my mate owes me a dance," Vohne declared.

Sarler noticed Kres only rolled his eyes, but he did allow the king to pull him onto the dance floor.

"*I arrived too slowly to save you.*" Saint pushed his way through the crowd and pressed his big head against Sarler's leg.

"That's okay. I'm all right."

The beast snorted. "*If you are fine then I will continue to hunt. Something smells delicious.*"

Before Sarler and Bleine could say anything, the big cat melted away into the crowd.

"I wonder what he's smelling," Sarler said.

Bleine shrugged. "I don't know. Hopefully it isn't something that'll get him in trouble. He causes enough just walking down the hall."

Sarler threw back his head and laughed. "True. So very true."

"Come dance with me, my love. After that, we can see if Kres will throw cake at Vohne."

"Why would he do that?" Sarler asked letting Bleine lead him into a gentle dancing motion.

Bleine smiled. "I can never figure it out but there's a fifty-fifty chance it will happen and the pictures are always worth blackmailing Vohne with later."

Sarler laid his head down on Bleine's shoulder. "You're right, we wouldn't want to miss that."

Cuddled up to his mate, Sarler enjoyed a rare, quiet moment dancing with the man he loved.

About the Author

Amber is one of those quiet people they always tell you to watch out for. She lives in Seattle with her husband, two sons, two cats and one extremely stupid dog.

Amber Kell loves to hear from readers. You can find her contact information, website details and author profile page at http://www.total-e-bound.com.

Total-E-Bound Publishing

www.total-e-bound.com

Take a look at our exciting range of literagasmic™
erotic romance titles and discover pure quality
at Total-E-Bound.